Three Outsiders

International Standard Book No: 0–936384–08–5
Library of Congress Catalog No: 82–083552
© 1983 by Cowley Publications
Published in the United States of America by Cowley Publications
cover design by James Madden, SSJE

THREE OUTSIDERS

pascal · kierkegaard
·Simone Weil

DIOGENES ALLEN

for Mary, George, John & Timothy

contents

Three Outsiders

THE SPIRITUAL LIFE TODAY

Many Christians are confused. Our churches offer a multitude of programs, such as Bible study, encounter groups, and retreats, which are supposed to contribute to the development of a spiritual life. But we do not have a very clear idea of what that is. A great deal is said about self-fulfillment and self-realization, but many of us have not thought very carefully about what these have to do with God. This question is explored by Georges Bernanos, the well-known French prewar novelist, in *The Diary of a Country Priest*. He portrays a stumbling, ridiculous-looking person whose earthly life is a failure but who is a true follower of Christ—his spiritual life is admirable. Christianity does promise happiness, an eternal happiness, but this is often confused with earthly success. This happiness is not divorced from our earthly lives, but how the connection is to be understood is not clear to very many people.

These remarks may sound arrogant, for how is it that I am an authority on spiritual matters? After all, I am not an extraordinary Christian, and presumably a person ought to be quite something spiritually to be able to speak with such confidence. Let me defend myself by making two points. First, the insights

I will use when speaking of the spiritual life are not my own but those of three writers—Blaise Pascal, Søren Kierkegaard, and Simone Weil. It is what I have learned from them that makes me aware of our lack of understanding of the spiritual life. Second, I personally have been looking for guidance and understanding in my own life. How am I to be a Christian—I who must go to work each day, who must raise and educate my children, who am middle-aged and with tastes greater than my income? I have been looking for some spiritual guidance and have found quite a lot in these three writers. They speak to our great aspirations and our frustrations, enabling us to understand why we live lives that are filled with boredom and frantic activity, and how we may become free from this bondage. Their conception of the spiritual life is developed in relation to our concern for personal fulfillment and the realization of our potential, neither endorsing nor rejecting out of hand our desire for happiness and well-being.

They also appeal to me because they are intellectually accomplished. Why does that matter? Well, I can read John Bunyan's classic *Pilgrim's Progress* and find ample spiritual guidance—trustworthy guidance, too. But the issue of the *truth* of the faith and the *basis* of the claims made is never really considered by him. He is strictly a practical guide, and not in any good sense of the word a theoretical one. A guide who is both theoretical and practical has developed some ideas of what God is, why he is hard to find, what people are, and why some people find God and others don't. He or she has some idea about the stages of Christian growth and the battles we ought to be fighting in order to become new creatures.

In short, in the writings of Pascal, Kierkegaard, and Weil we find a *theology*. Thus we can gain an understanding of ourselves and of our fellow creatures; we can get ideas about what

[4]

may impede our spiritual growth and that of other people; we can often discover what will enable us to develop further; we can learn to explain the reasonableness of what we are doing and to articulate the grounds of what we think and do.

Unfortunately the ideas of these three writers are not immediately accessible to many clergy, lay people, and students. Pascal's classic work was far from finished when he died. Because of its fragmentary state, it takes more time and study than most people can afford to discern the pattern in his thinking. In this book I lay out that pattern so as to enable those who have limited time to read Pascal himself with more profit. My aim is the same with Kierkegaard and Simone Weil. Kierkegaard is inaccessible because he wrote so much and often deliberately concealed his intentions. Simone Weil wrote beautifully, but because of the novelty of her vision, she is not easy to understand at first. I shall not try to present every aspect of these three writers, but I shall select only those which bear on our hunger for a full life.

Before we begin our examination something must be said about the setting in which the spiritual life is to be discussed. The spiritual life is not a timeless phenomenon; rather, it must be worked out in a specific time and place. In the early Christian centuries, for example, there were two factors to be taken into account: the revelation of God as presented by the apostles, and the existence of Rome—both as a political power and as a culture. Spirituality was worked out with both of these factors in play. So it is not accidental that early Christian spirituality, to use one example, placed so much emphasis on martyrdom. But for us today, the political ascendency of Rome is gone. With one factor missing, we have to make a very special effort to understand and appreciate early Christian spirituality.

The same is true of the Middle Ages. In the Middle Ages,

one focus was the church and the other, the barbarians. To impress the barbarians, it was necessary to show that Christianity enabled people to organize and sustain a way of life superior to their own. So Christianity was understood to have a strong public role. Later, the struggle was that of overlapping spheres of jurisdiction between the church and Christian rulers, which resulted in the idea of Christendom. The spiritual life was understood to a significant degree in terms of the role one was to play in a Christian society. But we do not have the barbarians, nor do we live in Christendom. Our present-day concerns have to do with an inherited Christianity and the modern emphasis on personal freedom. This stress on freedom began in the Renaissance and, after undergoing many changes, has become perhaps the dominant factor of our daily consciousness. Any realistic spirituality for today must take it into account.

Let me describe this ideal of freedom as it was voiced by Pico della Mirandola, a well-known Renaissance figure, in his *Oration on the Dignity of Man*. He pictures human beings as creatures filled with dignity because of their ability to be makers of their own destiny. Animals and plants are what they are and cannot be other than they are. But people are free. They may determine what they are to be: angels, apes, or anything that lies between these two extremes. So people have infinite possibilities for achievement and culture. There is a shift of attention from the salvation of our souls, which was dominant in the Middle Ages, to the realization of our human potential. The ideal of self-realization in the Renaissance took a literary and artistic direction, by and large, and the ideal was that of a cultivated courtier.

In the seventeenth century, Francis Bacon linked two ideas: the idea of humankind as creator of its destiny with the idea that knowledge is power. Knowledge of nature gives us power over nature. With such power we have the means to create our own future. We can determine our own destiny here on earth. Self-determination, or freedom to determine one's own destiny, became the ideal, and science the means of achieving our goals.

It is not accidental that in the last few years we have got ourselves into a rather depressed state, for we are getting signals that we are not after all in charge of our destiny on earth. We have come to recognize forces over which we do not have complete control. We are less confident that we can control our economies, or the technology we have created, or our tendency to use the power science has given us for waging war or for making the earth uninhabitable. The image of the sorcerer's apprentice, whose knowledge was limited so that the things he brought into being got out of control, has great plausibility as an image of our age.

Furthermore, every individual has applied to himself personally an idea which at first applied to the human race. The ideal at first was that the human race ought to be self-determining. People ought not to be victims of nature, but should be able to gain power over it and turn it into their servant. For us, however, it is not the *race* which ought to be master of its destiny, but I—the single individual. I ought to have what I want, to be what I want, to have my potential fulfilled, to have my consciousness satisfied. If I am not so catered to, then I am oppressed, I am violated, I am affronted, I am a victim.

This current malaise has its basis in a dream—the dream of the unlimited power of humanity to gain knowledge and control of all things, both in nature and in human nature. We almost took it for granted that the means for the attainment of our infinite possibilities and desires were available. Now that there are signs that the means are not available, we feel affronted and indignant. Someone is lying; new possibilities for fulfillment *must* be there somewhere. We have the built-in mechanism of a manic-depressive personality in the very ideal that was born in the Renaissance, linked to science by Bacon, and then applied to the individual instead of the race—self-realization and self-fulfillment for everyone through the unlimited and inevitable progress of science. When this seems possible, we are elated; when reality begins to break through, we are dejected. Rapid oscillation between the two renders us increasingly confused, anxious, and angry.

But modern science has always had two faces, like the Roman god Janus, looking in opposite directions. If, on the one hand, it pointed to potential human power over nature and thereby power to attain our goals, it also, from the very first, has had another face pointing in another direction, toward loss of meaning and significance. Our problem is not merely that of a sorcerer's apprentice whose limited knowledge unleashes forces which threaten to get out of control. If that were the only problem, then the answer would be *more* knowledge of nature and better technology. But the problem is deeper, and it was voiced by Pascal in the seventeenth century. On the one hand, human beings have greater appetites and greater aspirations than this world can fulfill; on the other, the new science gives no support to our assumption that human desires and aspirations matter. It reveals a universe that takes no account of people. It never tells us what is of inherent worth; it never reveals any purpose. As science progresses and brings more and more under its purview, human beings are left increasingly isolated in an alien universe. Today, they themselves are becoming an object of scientific study and are themselves becoming devoid of value and significance. We feel that we do indeed have significance that we are unable to sustain by our scientific knowledge.

Pascal was himself part of the new science, making first-rate contributions to it. Yet, at its very dawn, he saw with clarity and depth the other face of Janus. Pascal was not only rare in his day, but he saw what many working scientists and humanists of today still have not seen: that our progressive understanding of the world has been simultaneously a displacement of ourselves.[1] We do not know where we belong in the universe. We have become, as Pascal said, "an incomprehensible monster."[2]

So Pascal is not only a seventeenth century figure, but a contemporary—a person who is writing about *our* present plight. For our problem is that we do not know where we belong or what we are. Our sciences of nature and of people do not cohere with our sense of significance and worth. Only our religion supports this sentiment. Yet our religion seems to be discredited. This is why Pascal's first move is to reestablish the credibility of Christianity. He shows that Christianity has a profound and accurate understanding of people. Christianity thus deserves at least respect and careful consideration of what it tells us—who are confused—about people. From there he proceeds to show its ability to satisfy both the heart and mind.

So we shall begin with Pascal. But first let us note how all three writers I discuss in this book are relevant to our present plight. For all three are "outsiders." All three place themselves (at least in part of their work) on the threshold of the Christian church, and from that perspective address those inside. Christianity looks very different from this point of view and presents a challenge to those inside. The challenge may be illustrated by a story Kierkegaard tells about an insane man who has escaped from an asylum. As he walks along the road towards the town, he realizes that he will be recognized when he gets to town and forced to go back to the asylum. So he decides to say something that is true to the first person he meets, in order to prove to the townspeople that he is sane. So he says to the first person he meets, "The earth is round!" The townsman calls for help, the man is overpowered, and taken back to the asylum.

It is of course true that the earth is round, and what the Bible teaches about God may also be true. But Christian beliefs are frequently uttered in the wrong setting or situation. In the wrong place they too, by their bizarre quality, suggest imbalance. A sentence may be true; its utterance, a statement, may be quite unconvincing. All three writers want to teach us the appropriate way to utter Christian beliefs so that they may be soundly held and convincing. So they place themselves *outside* the normal precincts of the Church, that is, they look at human life as if it were apart from God. From this vantage point, they seek to provoke church people, who do have a commitment, to rethink the most simple, basic, and elementary truths of Christianity: that we are to love God and to love our neighbors, and to put these truths into play with our human and earthly thoughts, hopes, wishes, and desires. What church people are able to say before and after an encounter with these "outsiders" may be precisely the same words. But they are no longer uttered in the same way. We still hold to the assurance that our lives are in God's loving care, but not as though our lives follow a simple, upward course. The assurance of God's love is won through the turmoil and storms of life. These three writers, by standing outside the Church, enduring the cold darkness without the comfort of beliefs childishly held, can teach us so to hear and utter Christian truths as to find new and rich nourishment in them. So at times they make difficult and paradoxical remarks to move us toward the "hidden God." In that movement, our true life—the spiritual life—is revealed to us.

George Herbert, a seventeenth-century clergyman, composed a poem whose very organization illustrates the nature of the spiritual life. The lines of the poem run horizontally across the page just as in any other poem, but one word in each line connects diagonally with a word in the next line. Put together, these words read: "My life is hid in him who is my treasure"—an allusion to Colossians 3:3, "Your life is hid with Christ in God." So too, our daily lives are like the horizontal lines of the poem, with their own tales of successes and defeats. But those very lines contain, here and there, a single word, which when connected with other words tell another story. It is this story which these outsiders enable us to find, as we wrestle with the God who is hidden.

These three, who stand at the entrance, outside the Church, are not like most of those who are outside the Church. More will be said about their motivation when we consider each individually. But here I can say that they stand at the entrance because, from that point of view, they can help, not only those who are inside, but also those who are outside to enter. By examining human life apart from God, and then connecting Christian beliefs to that life, they can overcome profound misrepresentations of Christian teachings. All too often people outside the Church treat Christian beliefs in the wrong context, and this results in the kind of bizarreness Kierkegaard's story illustrates. This happens not intentionally nor maliciously, but because of the kind of ignorance which even learned and highly informed people can have when they deal with the things of God. For God is a "hidden God." One must not only know the right words, but learn how to think and speak in the right way. So Kierkegaard, Pascal, and Weil address those outside to correct their misunderstanding and to convert them; surprisingly, they frequently address them in the same way as they address those inside the Church. The one needs to learn for the first time, the other needs to be reminded, how to speak correctly about the things of God. They do not make the same mistakes, but from the point of view of those who stand at the doorway, both groups fail to wrestle sufficiently with the paradoxical truth that God is hidden.

Pascal, Kierkegaard, and Simone Weil clashed with institutional Christianity. Pascal closely aligned himself with Jansenism, a reform movement within the Roman Catholic Church, brilliantly defended it against the Jesuits, and was bitterly disappointed when it was condemned by the papacy. It was only after much soul-searching that he received the last rites of the Church on his deathbed. Kierkegaard went even further. He claimed that the Church had departed from genuine Christianity, and called upon the leaders of the Danish Church to admit it publicly. Because they ignored this challenge, Kierkegaard refused to receive the sacrament when fatally ill. Simone Weil remained unbaptized all her life, which meant she could not receive the host at Mass.

Institutions always have difficulty remaining faithful to their founding principles. If they are to be purified, they need to be challenged by those who are deeply and sincerely committed to the original vision. Pascal, Kierkegaard, and Weil do not seek to be destructive in their criticisms of institutional Christianity. Whether outside the Church or on its fringes, they are there because they want Christianity to be free of all that obstructs its witness to God.

They are much more out of line with the modern secular world. All three stress the need for submission, which collides violently with our ideal of freedom and self-determination. As I have pointed out, since the Renaissance we have progressively developed the idea of freedom in reference not only to the autonomy of the race but also to each individual, so that now the very idea of any authority to which one must submit is considered to be oppressive. Sartre goes so far as to claim that because we are free, there cannot be a God.

Christianity will inevitably appear to be hostile to human freedom. For even though it promises human fulfillment and eternal joy, it claims that to enter the kingdom of God requires an act of renunciation. Since the rise of modern science, which has led to unprecedented optimism concerning human possibilities on earth, Christianity seems to be too pessimistic over human nature and human possibilities. A better life has obviously been made possible by increasing scientific knowledge. Why submit to an alleged supernatural truth which calls for renunciation, and which at the same time is not verifiable by historical, scientific, or philosophical methods? By their uncompromising commitment to a hidden God, Pascal, Kierkegaard, and Weil stand opposed to some of the most powerful forces of Western culture.

They take their stand because of their devotion to the truth. They are not Christians because Christianity answers our desires and wishes, but because they honestly face our human condition and pierce the superficial optimism which claims that with more possessions, better education, better health, a longer life, and more personal liberty, human beings can be made happy. It is true that deprivation makes us miserable, but as all three show us, to have these things is not sufficient to make us happy. Only God can give us fullness because only he has an inexhaustible fullness. By yielding to him we can become free of our bondage to boredom, anxiety, and overdependence on things which cannot give us happiness. Instead of being against freedom, these writers show us how God can make us free.

The ideal of freedom in the modern world is symbolized by the supermarket, where we can choose what we want from a very large number of alternatives. The larger the range of choice, the more freedom we have. This is not a wholly erroneous view of freedom; for some choice is necessary for freedom. But it is an incomplete idea of freedom. Human beings need to be liberated from those things which keep them from seeking their own true good. Christianity teaches us how to become free of bondage so that we may freely yield ourselves to the greatest good, even at the loss of lesser goods.

The modern secular mentality, by its failure to consider anything which is beyond the intellect as real or true, has lost touch with that supreme good. Pascal, Kierkegaard, and Weil show us that because there is a superior reality, we may submit our minds and wills to it without doing violence to our intellect and without degrading ourselves.

PASCAL

In 1640, at the age of seventeen, Pascal made his debut as a mathematical prodigy with the first of his published works, and in a short time, he became widely recognized as a pioneer in the scientific revolution which gave us our modern physics. He showed a rare combination of theoretical and practical ability with his invention of the first calculating machine and his organization of a system of public transportation for Paris. Today, however, Pascal is remembered primarily for his unfinished apology for Christianity, a collection of fragments, called *Pensées*, which his early death prevented him from completing. He found his mathematical and scientific work easy in comparison with his examination of life apart from God and life lived by God's grace. This is perhaps worthy of note in our own age, when we marvel at displays of technical achievement and lament the relative lack of achievement in our understanding of the purpose and goals of human life.

Pascal's own religious life, along with that of his father and two sisters, was a conventional Roman Catholic one until the family became acquainted with the ideas of Augustine on grace. These ideas had been recently reinterpreted by Cornelius Jansenius, late Bishop of Ypres, and Pascal's family encountered them through the auspices of a parish priest. Jansenism, as this Catholic reform movement was called, had a stronghold in the monasteries of Port Royal. As a result of the family's greatly intensified piety, Pascal's younger sister, Jacqueline, became a nun at Port Royal in Paris the year after her father's death. Pascal, as his father before, opposed this largely for financial reasons. Intense conflict between newly-found piety and financial considerations apparently led him to a new awareness of the depths of his pride and selfishness. On November 23, 1654, Pascal had a powerful experience of direct contact with God during which the "hidden God" became manifest to him, and Pascal says that his conversion became total (F 913). It is the joy and certitude which he now knew which led Pascal to begin to write his apology, in hopes of leading others to the same happiness and certainty that he had found. His *Pensées* are characterized by the typical Augustinian radical contrast between humanity in its fallen state and human nature in a state of grace, but it is to Christianity which Pascal seeks to lead his readers, not to the specific outlook of the reform group he supported.

Pascal seems to have worked in great haste, writing down his thoughts on many slips of paper. By 1658 he was far enough along to give at least one address to his friends at Port Royal concerning his main arguments. In 1659 he began systematically classifying the nearly nine hundred fragments under twenty-eight headings, organizing nearly half of them in this way. But Pascal died before he could finish this classification, much less compose the projected book, and we have a great deal of difficulty determining precisely what Pascal's views were on many matters, since all we have is fragments only partly ordered. The fragments are even numbered differently in different editions and translations of the *Pensées*. Still, it is more profitable to study these fragments than most of the books that have been written on the nature of the spiritual life, and many of his views can be discerned.

The *Pensées* is a difficult book for other reasons. The structure of Pascal's thought is complex and delicately balanced. For example, he writes,

F 173   If we submit everything to reason our religion will be left with nothing mysterious or supernatural.

F 176   If we offend the principles of reason our religion will be absurd and ridiculous. Submission and the use of reason; that is what makes true Christianity.

F 170   *Submission.* One must know when it is right to doubt, to affirm, to submit. Anyone who does otherwise does not understand the force of reason. . . .

Pascal seeks to lead people towards the truth by affecting them at the deepest level of their personality. It takes some psychological discernment and experience of life to understand and appreciate many of his aphorisms.

F 98   How is it that a lame man does not annoy us while a lame mind [a fool] does? Because a lame man recognizes that we are walking straight, while a lame mind says that it is we who are limping.

He claims, moreover, that the truth cannot be grasped unless we are genuinely honest.

F 176   Those who do not love truth excuse themselves on the grounds that it is disputed and that very many people deny it. Thus their error is solely due to the fact that they love neither truth nor charity, and so they have no excuse.

Above all it is the fragmentary character of the *Pensées* which causes difficulty. All too often people who lack the time have dipped into them and, although impressed with his psychological and moral penetration, have failed to detect any pattern. His pungent remarks remain more or less isolated gems and the powerful case he makes for the truth of Christianity is not seen. I am concerned to make that pattern clear and thus make his view of the spiritual life accessible to those looking for guidance, spiritual nourishment, and conviction. Thus I do not cover every important aspect of the *Pensées,* but only enough to make the basic pattern of his argument clear.

1. Christianity Deserves Respect

Pascal's basic pattern of argument is summarized in a fragment which he placed in the first bundle of his papers.

F 12   Order. Men despise religion. They hate it and are afraid it may be true. The cure for this is to show that religion is not contrary to reason, but worthy of reverence and respect.

Next make it attractive, make good men wish it
were true, and then show that it is.
Worthy of reverence because it really under-
stands human nature.
Attractive because it promises true good.

This was written soon after Europe had been through the
devastation of the Thirty Years War (1618–48), a war between
Catholics and Protestants. This bitter conflict, as well as the
struggles for dominance between Catholics and Protestants in
France itself in the previous century, had discredited both creeds
in the eyes of many educated people. An attitude of thoughtless
pleasure-seeking and religious indifference developed among
the well-to-do, and this indifference was encouraged by the
witty observations on human folly and the insidious scepticism
of Montaigne's *Essays* (1595). This was the class of people that
Pascal had in mind. He wanted to break through the crust of
their indifference and to turn them into seekers after truth, so
that they would not only become interested in religion but come
to respect it. Pascal had something definite in mind by the term
"respect."

F 80   Respect means: put yourself out. . . . If respect
          meant sitting in an armchair we should be show-
          ing everyone respect and then there would be no
          way of marking distinction, but we make the dis-
          tinction quite clear by putting ourselves out.

So Pascal's first aim in his projected apology is to persuade
people "to put themselves out" by describing something that
will not allow them to continue to follow their customary and
habitual way of life. He seeks to win respect for Christianity

[19]

by showing its understanding of human nature. That understanding he displays in a series of paradoxes which show that we are a riddle to ourselves and do not understand what we are. On the one hand, we have reason and can achieve remarkable things; in making judgments, however, our reason is thrown off by the most irrelevant and insignificant factors.

> F 44   Would you not say that this magistrate, whose venerable age commands universal respect, is ruled by pure, sublime reason, and judges things as they really are, without paying heed to the trivial circumstances which offend only the imagination of weaker men? See him go to hear a sermon in a spirit of pious zeal. . . . If when the preacher appears, it turns out that nature has given him a hoarse voice and an odd sort of face, that his barber has shaved him badly and he happens not to be too clean either, then whatever great truths he may announce, I wager that our senator will not be able to keep a straight face.

More significantly jarring is the paradox that we who have such greatness can be utterly destroyed by the slightest imbalance in our bodies, or crushed as easily as an egg.

> F 200   Man is only a reed, the weakest in nature, but he is a thinking reed. There is no need for the whole universe to take up arms to crush him: a vapour, a drop of water is enough to kill him. But even if the universe were to crush him, man would still be nobler than his slayer, because he

knows that he is dying and the advantage the universe has over him. The universe knows nothing of this.

Thus we are both great and insignificant, and our greatness and insignificance do not fit together. They are disparate truths which no philosophical or psychological theory has been able to render compatible. One or the other extreme is stressed to the neglect of the other. With Plato and Descartes reason becomes our defining characteristic, so that we are not subject to nature; with Freud, on the other hand, our affective, irrational, animal side becomes our defining characteristic. The first theory stresses our greatness, the second our insignificance, yet neither theory can be sustained. For when we try to affirm our greatness, our lower selves and the vastness of the universe pull us from our lofty heights. When our insignificance is stressed, our distinctiveness from the rest of nature resists this evaluation. However small and irrational we may be, we are also able to become aware of our smallness and irrationality, so that our uniqueness cannot be utterly undermined by the vastness of space or the irrationality of our passions. But we cannot conclude that we are immensely significant because of the very smallness and irrationality of which we are aware. Our nature has both of these extreme features and, since they are incompatible, the inadequacy of philosophical and psychological theories which tend to go to extremes is not accidental. These extremes push us in opposite directions, so that as soon as we go in one direction, we are driven back toward the other. We cannot find a compromise by saying that we are neither great nor insignificant but something in between because we indeed are both great and insignificant, and these cannot be blended any more than can oil and water. Thus no philosophical or psychological theory can tell us what we are: great or insignificant.

But Christianity by its recognition of two levels of reality, the natural and the supernatural, can make sense of these extremes. According to Christianity, we are natural beings with a supernatural destiny. As natural beings we are limited and vulnerable, however much we exceed other creatures. We cannot base our greatness or significance on our *natural* endowments, because of our limitations and mortality, but a greatness based on our *supernatural* destiny is not affected by these. When we try to base our greatness on our natural powers, nature's size and majesty mock us. When our greatness is based on God's gift of an eternal life in his kingdom, it is not affected by nature or our natural limitations. God's gift as the basis of our greatness introduces a supernatural level into our understanding of human beings. It enables us to see how we are easily deflated insofar as we are natural beings, and yet how our greatness is secure insofar as we have a supernatural destiny.

As long as we stay on one level, the natural, we cannot find a resting place. We cannot know what we are or understand ourselves. But as soon as a supernatural level is introduced, we can understand the incompatible aspects of human nature. We can cease the vain attempt to determine what we are by staying on one level and being forced to go back and forth between two extremes. Our true nature includes a supernatural destiny, a greatness beyond the ceaseless see-saw because its basis is another level of reality (F 131).

Christianity also explains *why* we have the natural and conflicting features of greatness and insignificance. Our limi-

tations and vulnerability, which constitute the basis of our insignificance, and our reason and other powers which constitute
the basis of our natural greatness, are accounted for when viewed
from a supernatural perspective. As mere creatures we are limited and vulnerable as are all creatures in their different ways.
But we are creatures made in God's image. We are able to reason
and to relate to others on a personal basis. Our natural greatness
is seen as part of God's image, and that natural greatness has
been conferred on us to enable us to achieve our supernatural
destiny: to be related to God and to obey him freely.

We tend, however, to use our natural greatness for self-
elevation, ignoring the fact that we are great only because we
are made in God's image. So our natural greatness leads us to
pride, that is, to an attempt to base our status on our own
powers without any reference to God. Our natural powers thus
blind us to our true greatness, and God's good gift of natural
powers becomes a powerful barrier between us and God. We
therefore need to realize and constantly to be reminded that
our natural greatness is the result of our *supernatural* origin and
destiny. Our natural greatness, because it can fill us with pride,
must be tempered by an awareness of our limitations and vulnerability. It must be tempered by a knowledge of our insignificance in an infinite universe, the fallibility of our judgment,
and our susceptibility to microbes and viruses. Yet our insignificance cannot be allowed to take over completely, or we sink
into despair. The disparate features of our nature are to be used
to counter each other so that we neither become blinded by
pride nor sunk in despair. Ultimately, the incompatability of
our greatness and insignificance is so to baffle us as to open us
to a supernatural understanding of ourselves.

So a great many of Pascal's remarks are directed toward

either lowering us in our own estimation or raising us in our own eyes so that we become open to this supernatural understanding.

> F 130   If he exalts himself, I humble him. If he humbles himself, I exalt him. And I go on contradicting him until he understands that he is a monster [an anomaly] that passes all understanding.

Thus the incompatibility which prevents us from understanding ourselves as natural beings has its source in God. He desires to make creatures who can be related to him. Were we merely animals, we would not feel insignificant before the vastness of the universe. Because we are animals made in God's image, with a supernatural goal, it follows that we are a puzzle to ourselves, a puzzle no philosophical nor psychological theory can explain, as we have seen. Once Christianity has told us what we really are, however, we make sense to ourselves. We see why we have divergent aspects, and how we can make good use of the disparate features of our nature to keep ourselves from both pride and despair. For though we can learn much about ourselves from philosophy and psychology, neither one can resolve the riddle of our nature.

Christianity thus deserves respect. It should cause us to "put ourselves out," to seek God, if for no other reason than its understanding of human nature which presents such puzzling features. If we believe that various philosophies and psychologies are intellectually respectable and important because of the insights they give us about human beings, then in all fairness we ought to give serious attention to Christianity as well. On a strictly academic basis, it provides an illuminating explanation of the paradoxical features of our nature which neither philosophy nor psychology, while remaining on a natural level, are able to provide.

Pascal goes on to argue that Christianity alone faces squarely and genuinely the incompatible features of human nature. Other approaches tend to ignore one or the other. Even should they take some account of the duality, their solutions show that they do not fully face it. That is, they try to give us hope in the light of our obvious limitations and mortality by pointing to worthwhile and attainable goals. Such goals sell us short; we aspire to so much more than anything this world can give. This is clearly evident from our attitude toward our mortality. We want to live well and forever. The sacrifice we must make to accept lesser prospects as we would have to on any secular explanations, is itself testimony to the greatness of our aspirations. Christianity, however, never loses sight of either aspect of our nature, and the way both push us back and forth like a shuttlecock in our self-estimation. So we are never allowed to be lost in pride, sunk in despair, nor reconciled to life confined to earthly dimensions. It knows our greatness, a greatness far greater and more realistic than any greatness based on a prideful estimate of our nature.

This part of Pascal's argument—that Christianity is intellectually worthy of respect because of its understanding of human nature—is found in Reinhold Niebuhr in our century. Niebuhr in *The Nature and Destiny of Man* reviews intellectual history in the West, both ancient and modern, showing how every view of human nature either elevates us to pride or reduces us to animality and irrationality. He recommends Christianity for its realism in refusing to go to either extreme. His method of argument, as it reviews at length various philosophies, psychologies, and religions, is very different from Pascal's, since Pascal refers only in passing to such views. Pascal's method is a direct appeal to the reader by the use of paradox, which forces us to rise to a higher level to seek illumination. Both writers, however, show that Christianity has put its finger on certain truths about human nature. So although Christianity is not a psychological nor a philosophical theory about human nature, ignoring as it does many questions that these disciplines rightly and helpfully explore, it does call attention to their limitations. Because of human duality, no nonreligious account of human nature can be definitive. Our doubleness keeps pressing us to recognize that we live in a vast universe, that we are frail and mortal, and yet we have a stubborn sense of significance, a greatness which cannot be utterly suppressed by our smallness, fraility and mortality. Christianity keeps these hard facts ever before us, and helps to make us comprehensible to ourselves.

2. Christianity Is Attractive

The second part of Pascal's strategy is to show that Christianity is attractive. This is closely related to the previous part of his argument, for it includes the idea that human beings are incomprehensible to themselves apart from God. But it goes a step further by describing our attempts to evade an awareness of our condition. We hide from ourselves the wretchedness of our plight. Pascal summarizes our condition when we live apart from God as one of "inconstancy, boredom, anxiety" (F 24). Only one fact is needed to make us aware of our inconstancy.

F 43   A trifle consoles us because a trifle upsets us.

Were we more stable and more in control of ourselves, a trifle could not console us. That it does shows how easily we are upset. Boredom and anxiety are kept in check by constant activity.

F 136   A given man lives a life free from boredom by gambling a small sum every day. Give him every morning the money he might win that day, but on the condition that he does not gamble and you will make him unhappy. . . . Make him play for nothing; his interest will not be fired and he will become bored. . . . He must have excitement, he must delude himself into imaging that he would be happy to win what he would not want as a gift if it meant giving up gambling. He must create some target for his passions and then arouse his desire, anger, fear, for this object he has created. . . .

Even those who have the finest things in the world, if not distracted by activities, are likely not only to become bored but to start thinking of all the ways they can lose their possessions, or position, or people they care about, and of the possible diseases which may strike them, and death. Deprived of all activities which keep them from thinking about their condition, even well-placed people become anxious.

Pascal has no quarrel with our desire for excitement and possessions. What is erroneous is our assumption that in this way we shall be happy. Instead, it is all too obvious that once we have something we tire of it or want something else, and if we reflect for a moment, we know only too well that there is no way to achieve complete security.

> F 70   If our condition were truly happy we should not need to divert ourselves from thinking about it.

So Pascal tries to get people to look at their lives, to see that they know neither where they have come from, nor where they are going. Yet this matters, for they are going to die and their present activity does not give them complete and permanent satisfaction. Only a moment's pause and reflection is needed for them to realize that nothing they pursue can lead to fulfillment. It seems strange at first glance that what we know or can so easily realize about ourselves is kept from our awareness. But it is not really surprising that we keep it hidden from ourselves, since our condition is such a wretched one.

Christianity is attractive because it promises to release us from inconstancy, boredom, anxiety, and ignorance by showing us where to find happiness. It explains why we are miserable by its doctrine of original sin, and it points us to Christ who can remedy our faults and release us from our miserable condition. It leads us toward fullness of life, toward felicity in the truth and goodness of God.

The great barrier to happiness is our refusal to accept that we are at fault. The doctrine of original sin, the Christian explanation of our wretchedness, says that at the very center of our being we are in the wrong. We all admit that we have faults by the very fact that we seek to improve ourselves. We concentrate on various traits in our personalities—a tendency not to listen, a tendency to overeat, a tendency to be jealous, a tendency to grow angry, and all the rest—seeking to improve this or that fault. But the trouble is deeper than this. Our entire persons are at fault, not this or that aspect of ourselves. We are in a condition or state of "being in the wrong."

We balk at this not only because of a reluctance to admit that at the core of our being we are sinners, but because at first it is implausible to say that our wretchedness is our own fault. The story of Adam and Eve tells us that the first parents of the human race disobeyed God and by that act the whole human race is in a condition of sin. How can we take this seriously? Are we to take it as literal history? That is highly implausible today. Are we perhaps to say that there were no such people as Adam and Eve? All we can say is that at some time in evolutionary history, humans came into being and obeyed God and all went well. At a later time people ceased to obey God and then disobedience spread like an infection, so that now we all live in a fallen state.

To determine whether this is "true" or not is not the real issue. The stumbling block is that there is no way for us to understand how people who are utterly free of evil can ever commit an evil act, think an evil thought, or speak an evil word. This is what makes the notion of sin as a radical fault at the core of human beings, for which they are responsible, so difficult to understand. What would cause someone utterly free of evil to do wrong? People can only be tempted to do wrong if they are *already* attracted to evil, and therefore already less than utterly good. So it is not a matter of finding in early human history the existence of a paradise and a fall from it to establish the truth of the Christian doctrine of original sin.

This was recognized explicitly by Augustine, who even though he believed in an historic Adam and Eve, saw clearly that the real issue lay in the very incomprehensibility of sin itself. How can those who are in a state of goodness act wrongly when there is no reason whatsoever in their makeup to lead them to disobedience? People act for reasons; they have motives. Thoroughly good people have no reason to do wrong. To say that Adam and Eve wanted to be their own God tells us nothing about where they got the evil motive for that act. The story of Adam and Eve, instead of telling us how evil first began, forcefully puts before us the *nature* of sin by stressing that Adam and Eve were in Paradise, were created good and lived in harmony with God, and yet *unaccountably* succumbed to temptation. So the Christian doctrine of original sin tells us that we are in a condition of wretchedness because we are not obedient to God, and that we are responsible for this condition, but it does not tell us how we got there in the first place. So it is reasonable for us to balk at first over acceptance of the Christian explanation of our wretchedness because sin is incomprehensible. We cannot understand how anyone could or can go from a condition of utter goodness into sin, or indeed how we ourselves have done so (F 131, 431).

Goethe in *Faust* expresses this incomprehensibility by contrasting the slowness of the body to the quickness of the mind. The transition from one place to another by the body, he says, is vastly slower than the transition from one thought to another. But actually our thinking is very slow when compared to the transition from good to evil. It is instantaneous: we move from one to the other without anything in between. Thus the story of Adam and Eve, and so too the Christian doctrine of original sin, tell us that human beings are responsible for their present wretchedness—their inconstancy, boredom, and anxiety—because of a fault at the core of their being. But the story and the doctrine are not about the *genesis* of sin. We are not told how we move from good to evil. Sin—going from good to evil—is incomprehensible. But our condition is one in which we have that fundamental fault.

Even though we do not understand how sin arose or arises, the Christian doctrine of sin is illuminating. It tells us that we are unhappy because we do not obey God, but live without him. Without this reason, our wretchedness remains incomprehensible to us; for we are unhappy in a peculiar way.

F 117　　Who would think himself unhappy if he had only one mouth and who would not if he had only one eye? It has probably never occurred to anyone to be distressed at not having three eyes, but those who have none are inconsolable.

F 116　　All these examples of wretchedness prove his greatness. It is the wretchedness of a great lord, the wretchedness of a deposed king.

Our unhappiness is such that it points beyond itself to greatness and the greatness it points to is a supernatural, not a natural, one. Earlier we saw that an assessment of our nature solely in terms of our natural endowments causes us to oscillate continuously between a sense of greatness and a sense of insignificance. From a higher perspective, we have a greatness revealed which is not subject to such oscillation because it is not diminished by our weaknesses or limitations. Now some of the unhappiness we suffer is similar to that suffered by those who once were great but now are fallen, of those who have lost what they once had and now are inconsolable. For ordinary people to feel this kind of wretchedness makes no sense from a natural perspective. But from a higher perspective it does:

[31]

the perspective which says that our happiness is to be found in obedience to God. Through our failure to obey we are wretched, subject to inconstancy, boredom, and anxiety, needful of diversions to keep us from thinking about and feeling our wretchedness.

3. *Christianity Is True: The Three Orders*

Pascal's third goal is to show that Christianity is true. When in fragment 12 he announces his other two goals—to show that Christianity is worthy of respect and to make it attractive—he indicates briefly how he is to achieve those aims. It is worthy of respect because it enables us to understand human nature; it is attractive because it promises true good. But Pascal gives no indication whatsoever of how he is going to accomplish the third goal, to show that Christianity is true. There is no way for him to state his method briefly, and also in accomplishing his first two goals Pascal is well on his way to showing that Christianity is true.

In each of the previous two stages he has employed and rendered plausible his fundamental conviction about two distinct levels of reality. As we saw, Pascal shows us that we are both great and insignificant, great and wretched. These "contradictions" give us over to turmoil and tension. The questions they raise are not remote but are directly concerned with our nature and condition, and their paradoxical truth can be recognized by an intelligent person with only a moment's honest reflection. The truth is sometimes present within the fragment itself because each side of the opposition shows that the other is true.

F 114   It is wretched to know that one is wretched, but there is greatness in knowing one is wretched.

So the first part of his method of showing that Christianity is true is to confound us with paradoxes about ourselves so that we are baffled as to what our true nature is. We are driven by paradoxes not only to recognize, but also to feel, the incomprehensibility of our nature and the wretchedness of our condition. The second part of his argument shows that what is incomprehensible to us apart from Christianity makes sense from a supernatural perspective. So Pascal uses paradoxes which cannot be resolved on one level to pressure us to rise to another level for illumination. He moves us toward submission to the truth of Christianity by showing to our reason its own limitations as well as the intellectual illumination that Christian truth gives to the mind. Without Christian truth there is oscillation from one side of the paradox to the other, and unending bafflement. We are thus shown by our reason the place where reason should submit and yield itself to Christian truth.

Reason cannot discover supernatural truth—the truth that we are created in God's image, fallen, and redeemable. These are revealed to us in Scripture by God's inspiration to chosen people. But to expect a response of faith to Christian truth *before* our reason is led to see the paradoxes about ourselves and recognize the wretchedness of our condition would be to subject reason to tyranny. The proper response to Christian truth is indeed one of faith, but only after we grasp with our reason the facts of our incomprehensibility and our wretchedness. Only

[33]

then can we see by reason the coherence which results from Christian truth, giving us as it does an understanding of those paradoxes which without Christian truth utterly baffle our reason and leave us in our wretchedness without hope of remedy. Even though faith is not produced by reason, our faith is reasonable because Christian truth illumines our intellect on matters which otherwise baffle us. The study of human nature by reason is essential, because without it our intellect would not receive illumination from the Christian truths we hold by faith. Without such study and illumination, submission to Christianity (faith) is improper—based on false foundations, such as craven fear or the mistaken idea that Christianity promises earthly rewards.

> F 172　The way of God, who disposes all things with gentleness, is to instil religion into our minds with reasoned arguments and into our hearts with grace, but attempting to instil it into hearts and minds with force and threats is to instil not religion but terror.

Faith is thus not blind when it comes *after* reason has examined our nature and condition, and the intellect is illumined by Christian truth.

This much of Pascal's argument for the truth of Christianity is present in the first two steps of his apology, those which show that Christianity is to be respected and that it is attractive.

There is an additional feature of Pascal's case for the truth of Christianity. Pascal actually distinguishes three levels of reality, dividing the natural into two categories. He calls these three levels three "orders" because each has its own faculty of ap-

prehension, its own objects of importance, and its own principles of judgment. Each order gives rise to a distinctive kind
of life.

The first level is that of the body, which is called "carnal"
in the biblical sense of "flesh" and includes our wishes, desires,
and even our minds insofar as they are disobedient to God.
Our desires are for worldly possessions and power. Its faculty
is the senses, to the degree that the senses cause us to judge
things by their external appearance. This is the level of kings
and politicians, who are dominated by a desire for power, and
of the rich and would-be rich who are dominated by a concern
for external appearances, but all of us are affected by this order
to a degree and at times decisively.

Pascal recognizes that this level has its own sort of greatness and achievements, pointing out that societies rely on this
level of motivation to make successful the organizations and
institutions which give us a degree of order and security. He
pays it a back-handed compliment with his wry remark:

F 106   Greatness. Causes and effects show the greatness
        of man in producing such excellent order from
        his own concupiscence.

This level or order is unable to perceive the greatness of
the next level, that of the mind.

F 308   The greatness of intellectual people is not visible
        to kings, rich men, captains who are all great in
        a carnal sense.
        Great geniuses have their power, their splen-
        dour, their greatness, their victory and their lustre,

and do not need carnal greatness, which has no relevance for them. They are recognized not with the eyes but with the mind, and that is enough.

Pascal as a mathematical genius and as a pioneer in the rise of modern science clearly admires the greatness of this level. He shows his respect for it by his insistence that faith, which is on a higher level, must not exercise "tyranny" over reason, but for religious truth to awaken a proper faith, the intellect must be illumined and thus satisfied.

The third level Pascal designates as the order of the heart, for the heart is its faculty. Its objects are holiness and wisdom, its principle of judgment is charity.[3] This level has its own greatness which is distinct from the other two, and a greatness not accessible to the senses and the mind, the faculties of the other two orders. At this level the heart must be used to appreciate the greatness of holiness and divine wisdom.

> F 308   Jesus without wealth or any outward show of knowledge has his own order of holiness. He made no discoveries; he did not reign, but he was humble, patient, thrice holy to God, terrible to devils, and without sin. With what great pomp and marvelous magnificent array he came in the eyes of the heart which perceive wisdom!

Just as the first level is primarily concerned with the senses, and the second with the mind, the third is primarily concerned with the will, its direction and motivation, and thus primarily with charity or love. The truth which concerns the divine love which redeems us and enables us in turn to love is the truth or wisdom which charity values. Charity cannot be procured from the realities which make up the other two levels.

F 308   Out of all bodies together we could not succeed in creating one little thought. It is impossible, and of a different order. Out of all bodies and minds we could not extract one impulse of true charity. It is impossible, of a different, supernatural order.

Charity can be produced only by divine action, by the gracious spirit of God at work in us, or as Pascal puts it, by inspiration.

All we can learn about the supernatural order while we are within the boundaries of the other two levels, and have our understanding directed by their standards, is the *effects of its absence.* The level of human desires and wishes, the level of possessions and the exercise of power, without charity becomes corrupt and hence is called the domain of "flesh."

Pascal is not concerned to portray human perversity, sordidness, and cruelty—which are abundantly clear to all of us anyway. Instead he is concerned with the way our psychological endowment can be so formed as to be similar to a habit. We then would act, think, and feel automatically, just as we behave in a habitual way when we become accustomed to act in a certain way through continual repetition. Thus our flight from thinking about our condition and our constant search for excitement, novelty, new possessions and achievements, as though happiness can be found in this way, in time forms our character so that we become bounded by it. Pascal refers to our character as "the Machine" because our behavior and passions have become as automatic as the operations of a machine. We cannot then respond to higher truths, especially Christian truths, when we encounter them. They bore us and seem to be mere platitudes. Acts of charity and holiness become pearls cast before swine.

Even should the barrier created by our "fleshly" character be pierced by Christian truth, which is possible, it continues to cause us great difficulty. We find it hard to remain constant in our conviction of the truth of Christianity. The passions—our wishes, wants, desires, hopes, ambitions, aims—are so worldly that Christian charity does not satisfy them, does not provide food for them. So God makes contact with only a small part of us. Since it is the presence of divine charity—the presence of God's spirit—which gives us assurance and conviction regarding the reality of the supernatural realm, we are inconstant in this conviction. A part of us may want to believe, but we find ourselves more often unable to believe or to believe with conviction, even though we are not particularly troubled by any intellectual objection to the truth of Christianity. So it is that the passions, on a level below that of reason, can cause unbelief and doubt. From the amount of attention Pascal devotes to the passions, to the "machine," he appears to think that the passions, not reason, are the most important source of indifference toward Christianity.

Pascal's solution for this doubt about supernatural truth is the reeducation of the passions by repetitive action. Just as habits are formed by repetition, habits can be broken and new ones formed by repetition. So he advises people to go to church, to pray, to "go through the motions" just as if they were full of conviction even when they feel they are getting nowhere. In time the passions will become re-formed, accompanied by a greater openness to divine charity, and such people will find that their hunger grows and their appetite is satisfied by the food of divine love.

It is at the first level, that of the passions, and in relation to "the machine" that Pascal's famous Wager Argument must be understood. In a long fragment that Pascal himself did not classify under his twenty-eight selected headings, it is argued on the analogy of gambling that the odds greatly favor betting on the existence rather than on the nonexistence of God. If God does exist, the payoff is infinitely great (F 148).

It is often thought both by supporters and critics that this is the basis on which Pascal recommends Christianity for belief, some defending and others raising moral objections to such a reason for belief. Actually the context of the Wager Argument must be considered, for it is proposed to an imaginary person who is a gambler and who does not believe in Christianity. Pascal wants to show the gambler through an analogy he can appreciate that he has no *intellectual* ground on which to reject Christianity. Both Pascal and his imaginary interlocutor agree that we are incapable of knowing by reason alone whether God exists or what he is. But the possibility of a Christian God matters infinitely as far as our well-being is concerned. In these circumstances the intelligent thing to do, Pascal proceeds to argue, is to wager that God exists. Immediately after the unbeliever is convinced by Pascal that he ought to believe, he exclaims, "I am being held fast and I am so made that I cannot believe. What do you want me to do?" To which Pascal answers,

F 418   That is true, but at least get it into your head that, if you are unable to believe, it is because of your passions, since reason impels you to believe and yet you cannot do so. Concentrate then not on convincing yourself by multiplying proofs of God's existence but by diminishing your passions. You want to be cured of unbelief and you ask for the remedy: learn from those who were once bound like you and who now wager all they have. . . . They behaved just as if they did believe, taking holy water, having masses said, and so on. That will make you believe quite naturally. . . .

The Wager Argument is thus used to show to a particular kind of person who does not believe that it is his passions, not intellectual reasons, which hinder his belief, and Pascal offers him a way to overcome this particular barrier to belief. So the Wager Argument belongs to the level of the "flesh," which is below the level of the mind.

On the level of the mind we can become aware that we are both great and insignificant, without being able to understand why, and that we are wretched without being able to find a remedy. This is the effect of the absence of the supernatural. We cannot understand ourselves precisely because we have a supernatural origin and our well-being depends on our proper relation to the supernatural level. We cannot by our intellect discover Christian truth, but our intellect can make us aware that we cannot make sense of ourselves nor find happiness.

F 242   Any religion which does not say that God is hidden is not true, and any religion which does not explain why does not instruct. Ours does this. "Verily thou art a God that hidest thyself."

We can see why Pascal says that God is hidden. He is not to be grasped by our senses, so he is hidden in that respect, and he is hidden because he does not satisfy those who seek power, dominance and worldly distinction. Those who seek him by these means, or who are dominated by them, cannot perceive the greatness, goodness, and the attraction of Jesus and the saints. The things of God give them no satisfaction, yet God is present to them even in his absence. The wretchedness they feel and which they must constantly endeavor to keep at bay is caused by their lack of knowledge of the spiritual realm. They cannot reach it by their senses or receive it through their worldly passions, but its reality exerts its effect on them by its very absence.

God is hidden also from those who seek him through their minds alone; the supernatural level is the level of charity, not intellect. Frequently intellectual world views have been constructed in which God is an essential ingredient to their coherence, as in the case of Deism in the eighteenth century, which set itself up as a rival to Christianity (F 449). According to Deism, God's existence was required by the very existence and design of nature. Since the time of Hume and Kant, however, demonstrations of God's existence have been regarded at best as highly questionable by most philosophers. For Pascal himself these demonstrations and intellectual constructions do not give us access to God, or only in rare cases. Without charity we do not know God (F 189, 190–2). To know him, we need contact with him. So just as it is tyrannical to make reason submit to faith before the intellect discovers our incomprehensibility and our wretchedness, so too is it tyrannical to seek to reach God without faith. Faith cannot be a proper faith until our reason discovers our incomprehensibility and our wretchedness, for human nature must be taken into account.

[41]

As Pascal sometimes puts it, in demonstrations and intellectual constructions we seek to reach God without recognizing the need of a mediator; that is, without a recognition of our wretchedness and our need for a savior (F 190).

God is indeed evident from the existence and order of nature to those who know their own wretchedness as well as divine charity. So we must think in the correct sequence to keep from confounding different levels of reality; if we do not, God is absent even in those intellectual constructions in which he is said to be present. What is known is reduced to the level of mind; the greatness of God cannot be contained in our constructions.

Although the supernatural level is beyond the natural, as we have seen, the intellect performs several indispensable services. It can show us that we are riddles to ourselves, and that Christianity makes sense of our nature and condition. Through our reason we can distinguish three orders and show why Christianity is so easily dismissed by those who look for the greatness which is merely external, or the greatness of our various sciences which are of the intellect alone. The greatness of Christianity has to do with charity, and the wisdom which belongs to the order of charity. By our intellect we can see that to come to a proper faith we must reason in such a way as to respect the distinctions between the three orders. By performing these services, the intellect shows us that to gain enlightenment we must look to Scripture which contains supernatural truth, and that for us to receive faith and charity we must humbly wait for God's action. Thus, the mind shows that to submit our intellect to Christian truth and ourselves to God is not contrary to reason nor destructive of our personality. Only by a proper submission may we find relief from our ignorance and a remedy for our misery; only so shall we find that truth and goodness which can give us happiness.

The existence of three levels, or orders, accounts for both the clarity and the obscurity of Scripture through which supernatural truth is revealed. God is essentially hidden because he is a supernatural reality, not to be grasped by our senses and incapable of being fully portrayed by any mental construction. The life he seeks to give us is also supernatural, so that our happiness can be represented only by "figures." Thus when God reveals supernatural truth, it is hidden in the sense that the truth cannot be grasped by an understanding dominated by worldly desires and aims, nor by the intellect alone—since this truth is presented to us symbolically. Only people who recognize their plight can find enlightenment.

God reveals himself obscurely because he seeks to redeem us with our cooperation and not by means of tyranny. If God revealed himself with earthly greatness, he would win us over in a worldly way; if he sought to win us over by a display of his truth that was nonfigurative and hence without obscurity, our intellect would assent but we would still be devoid of charity.

> F 234   God wishes to move the will rather than the mind. Perfect clarity would help the mind and harm the will.
> Humble their pride.[4]

God does not exercise such tyranny over us, but wins our allegiance by the recognition by our intellect of our need for supernatural enlightenment and help, and by our desire for the greatness of charity. His revelation through the Scriptures

[43]

is thus both clear and obscure. It provides enough light to find God for those who desire him, who desire a good beyond the earthly and a charity beyond the domain of the mind. But there is not enough light to make us proud; that is, to make us think that there is really nothing which is beyond our powers to know and reach, so that we do not have to rely utterly on the grace of another for the knowledge which enables us to understand ourselves and for our happiness.

> F 446   If there were no obscurity man would not feel his corruption: if there were no light man could not hope for a cure. Thus it is not only right but useful for us that God should be partly concealed and partly revealed, since it is equally dangerous for man to know God without knowing his own wretchedness as to know his wretchedness without knowing God.

The Bible gives sufficient light because it tells us in myriad ways that God has called a people, Israel, and made to it great promises. We see from history that there is a Jewish people, whose descendents are still with us and who hold to those promises. We have a witness that these promises are misunderstood when taken in a carnal way, for an earthly Israel is not all that was promised. Israel is a figure or type or symbol of a greater kingdom to come; the earthly kings of Israel, especially David and Solomon, are figures and types of a greater king who is to come. This basic line of scriptural witness is hard fact to Pascal, and so too are the Old Testament prophecies and their fulfillment in Christ. In short, the basic Christian story of creation, fall, promise, and fulfillment is clearly discernible in Scripture to those who can see a good beyond this world and whose minds recognize that charity is beyond the intellect.

For people whose desires are merely worldly, the Bible has no appeal whatsoever. For people who employ the intellect only, historical study reveals so much that is obscure and doubtful that the Bible's claims cannot be made good. For those who recognize how mysterious we are to ourselves, who recognize and feel our wretched condition, it provides illumination and the hope of remedy in spite of all its obscurities and its incapacity to be set on a firm and unquestionable basis by historical or philosophical reasoning alone.

Those truths which belong to the domain of the mind can be known and affirmed without a consideration of our human condition. In mathematics, Pascal's favorite field, the truth of a particular mathematical proposition can be made evident on the basis of some axioms, theorems, and rules of deduction without taking into account our own incomprehensibility to ourselves or our plight. But the truths revealed by Scripture are not clear enough to be demonstrable by reason alone because they do not belong to the domain of the mind. Their truth is thus not evident to our minds alone. They must be considered by the mind *of a person*, and in particular the mind of a person who recognizes his or her incomprehensible nature, his or her insufficiency, his or her plight. So the truths revealed in Scripture are not enough to convince the mind working abstractly; they are convincing only to the mind of a person who is driven to search by a knowledge of his or her ignorance and misery.

Although the Bible is obscure, it provides enough illumination to judge those who do not know God, for they could find him by following its light if they wanted to. It is because they lead thoughtless lives, engaged in innumerable diversions, that they do not seek God. They seek relief from their emptiness or distress in human wisdom only—from medicine, psychology, philosophy, and the like. They do not face the reality of their own persons. For them the witness of Scripture is never enough, never plausible enough, never clear enough, never sufficiently compelling. They point to those things in Scripture which are obscure in order to justify their ignoring those things in Scripture which are clear. Thus the light sent to guide and help them, instead of bringing them relief, judges them. It reveals their errors, reveals that they are in the wrong. However obscure, it is clear enough to leave them without excuse (F 427, 449).

The scriptural witness which illumines the intellect of a person able to appreciate it does not, however, give us love. This can occur only when we are touched by the gracious presence of God, and thereby can rise to the order of charity. This is beyond the reach of the order of the mind, and even beyond the reach of the mind illumined by the supernatural truth that Scripture reveals. The principle of the supernatural order is charity, so to know God is to have contact with his graciousness and to be ruled by it.

4. *The Nature of Faith*

We need to clarify the status of faith as a basis for belief before we consider the supernatural nature of charity. Pascal's apology in which he uses reason to show us our own incomprehensibility leads us to look to a higher level for understanding. It is necessary for reason to do this if faith is to be a proper faith. Otherwise the intellect is not satisfied, and any faith we had would be a blind one. But the reasoning procedure followed, and the illumination Christian truths give us by their explanation of our condition, do not give us faith. Faith is the result of the presence of God, of his grace at work in us (F 7, 424). This is often said but easily ignored, so that faith often gets treated as though it belongs to the natural order. We can expose this error and avoid it, as well as better understand the nature of faith as a basis for making religious affirmations, by distinguishing two approaches. Kierkegaard, whose views on this are the same as Pascal's, calls them the way of objectivity and the way of subjectivity.

The way of objectivity is Pascal's domain of the mind, in which we reason and consider evidence without taking into consideration our human nature or our plight. When Christianity is approached in this way, should the evidence for Christianity be conclusive, we will of course believe that the claims made by Christianity are true. If the evidence is conclusive, then faith is not needed, since we will know its claims are true. Following this approach further, should the evidence not be sufficient to establish Christian claims, then faith is said to be needed in order to affirm them. Faith is used to hurdle the gap between the claims and the evidence. But if the gap is rather large, then many people would conclude that to have faith is irrational.

This is precisely what many people today think the situation is: the gap is too large between Christian claims and the evidence for their truth, so that it is unreasonable to have faith. People may believe if they want to, but an intellectually honest person who is not swayed by emotions would not. Some people consider the gap to be large because the traditional proofs for God's existence from the very existence of the universe and

[47]

from its order have been shown by modern philosophy to rest on highly questionable assumptions. It is also claimed that we cannot infer that God exists from religious experience, since something else might be the cause of the experience. Biblical criticism cannot establish that God revealed himself to the Jews or in Jesus Christ. This is of course to paint with very broad strokes, but it is sufficient to make the main point. Faith is treated as a way to overcome the gap between Christian claims and the evidence, and many people for the sort of reasons I have mentioned, think the gap is too large to be reasonably bridged by faith.

Still following the way of objectivity, if the gap is not too great, and many people today think it is not, then it is all right to step over or leap the gap. They too regard faith as if it were a supplement for evidence. They go as far as the evidence will take them, and then they turn to faith as a substitute for evidence. Should they be challenged for this reliance on faith in place of evidence, they reply with examples of many other beliefs we have in various academic and scientific disciplines, and daily activities in which we make assumptions which we cannot certify with evidence. It is argued that since it is permissible elsewhere, it is permissible in religion. If this is accepted, then their opponent must then rely solely on the largeness of the gap to be bridged. We are then left with two rival positions: one claiming the gap is too large to be bridged by faith; the other sure that it is sufficiently narrow to be so bridged. But both treat faith as a way of bridging a gap between claims and evidence for the claims.

The way of objectivity is the wrong way to approach religious claims, however valid it may be with other claims. It is improper because it puts religious truths on the wrong level by reducing them to the level of natural truths. Consequently, when the evidence is not sufficient to establish them, religious faith is seen as a substitute for evidence. So too those who think that the gap between Christian claims and the evidence is small, treat faith as a substitute for evidence.

The objective way leaves out of consideration the mind of the *person* who examines Christian claims. It assumes that all people given the same data—if they are intelligent, responsible, and trained to investigate and evaluate data—will come to the same conclusion, more or less. The fact that we are incomprehensible to ourselves and that our condition is wretched is considered *not* to be a necessary part of the awareness of a person who is evaluating Christian claims or coming to faith. It is not even considered to be relevant.

The mistake can be illustrated by the following analogy. Water will feel hot, cold, or lukewarm to a hand depending not only on the temperature of the water, but also on the temperature of the hand. The temperature of the hand is relevant to how the water feels. Likewise, the condition of the person making an evaluation of Christian claims is essential to that evaluation. The condition includes not only the degree of training, fairmindedness, and the like, but also that individual's awareness of the true human condition, incomprehensible and wretched. Thus the way of objectivity reduces Christian truth to the natural order by ignoring or dismissing the significance of our condition as human beings as we make the evaluation. When Christian truths are viewed as belonging to the same plane as all other truths, then faith is of course treated as bridging the gap between the claims and the evidence for the claims, and so as a substitute for evidence.

Pascal, Kierkegaard, and Weil approach Christian truths in another way. Kierkegaard calls it the way of subjectivity, which refers to the human subject, not to bias or personal prejudice. This approach considers the *condition of the person* as essential. For unless we are puzzled about our own nature and aware of our plight, Christian truths do not illumine our minds and meet our needs. The reasons or grounds for affirming Christian truths must include the illumination and nourishment given by Christian truths, or else Christian claims are reduced to a natural plane. Otherwise faith becomes a substitute for evidence in the evaluation of Christian claims. Pascal believes that faith arises by the action of God (F 7, 424). If we are open to the illumination Christian truth bestows and earnestly seek a remedy for our wretchedness, we can be moved by God's grace to faith. "The heart has its reasons of which reason knows nothing" (F 423). We affirm Christian truths not because we have made a leap from evidence to assent, but because we have been acted on by God and find ourselves confessing that Jesus is Lord. "No one can say 'Jesus is Lord' except by the Holy Spirit" (I Cor. 12:3). "You will find him, if you search after him with all your heart and with all your soul" (Dt. 4:29b).

The objective approach misunderstands the nature of faith and cheapens it by treating it as an inferior substitute. Rather, faith is a gift of God, a response to supernatural truth by those who earnestly seek illumination and relief.

There is another aspect to faith which can be called secondary faith. Since we presently do not see all things under the rule of Christ, we are to have faith that all is under his authority and that his rule will eventually become manifest, that his kingdom will come. Such a faith is secondary faith; for it is based and grounded on the primal faith awakened in us by God. Secondary faith, because it leaps beyond what is presently knowable, has a superficial affinity to believing something by faith because one cannot affirm it solely by evidence. God's authority over all is affirmed even though it is not fully evident to us, and Christ's rule over all is affirmed even though it is not yet here. But such faith differs from a view of faith as a substitute for evidence, because it is a *secondary* faith. That is, its basis is a primary faith, a faith resulting from divine grace and sustained by God's action.

Pascal's apology for the credibility of Christianity has faith as its crown, the faith of an intellect which has learned when to yield to what is beyond its domain. He leads us into a realm or order whose governing principle is love, but he himself does not explore it. So we will now turn to Kierkegaard's *Works of Love*, which has the second of the great commandments, "Love thy neighbor as thyself," as its theme. Then we will examine the writings of Simone Weil for their contribution to our understanding of the first of the two great commandments, "Thou shalt love the Lord thy God." We examine them in this order because it is by obedience to the second commandment that we become better able to obey the first.

KIERKEGAARD

In Kierkegaard's time, the first half of the nineteenth century, the social and intellectual climate was favorably disposed toward Christianity. The essentially hostile attitude of the Enlightenment thinkers such as Voltaire and Kant, who came after Pascal, was no longer in fashion. The Enlightenment's cold and narrow view of reason, within whose bounds it sought to confine religion, was replaced on the one hand by Romanticism, which reintroduced the mysterious, the exotic, and the passionate, and on the other hand by Hegelianism. Hegel attacked the Romantic stress on mystery and thought it overrated spontaneity. Nonetheless, Hegel himself exhaustively explored the depths of human consciousness and created a powerful new synthesis of human knowledge under the category of Spirit. Religion was an essential part of the human spirit for both the Romantic and the Hegelian, and Christianity was considered to be the highest form of religious expression.

Kierkegaard stood outside the general and somewhat patronizing approval of Christianity. He believed that Christianity as presented was a version so tamed and domesticated that its demand for radical and decisive choice was completely concealed. Kierkegaard did not have to overcome an attitude of hostility or one of indifference toward Christianity, as Pascal did, but an attitude of condescension. Everyone thought he or she knew what Christianity was and nearly everyone was a Christian as a matter of course, just as everyone was a citizen of his or her native land as a matter of course. So Kierkegaard sought to make the distinctive and extraordinary nature of Christianity unmistakably clear, sometimes by means of writing books under pseudonyms, often claiming the identity of a non-Christian or one who was not able to understand Christianity. In a daring and provocative way he attempted to put Christianity before the eyes of his contemporaries as a creed whose claims present an absolute paradox to human reason and a personal challenge to every individual. As far as Kierkegaard is concerned, unless we have seen the challenge of Christianity and stood before it in fear and trembling, we have not understood Christianity. Once we have seen what Christianity is, we can never think it ordinary nor ever again go about our business as before.

Kierkegaard, who could be utterly fascinating and charming in society, was nonetheless in his day an oddball. He circulated not only in the best Danish society, but also with artists, actors, and intellectual Bohemians. For all his high spirits and sense of fun in public, he was not a playboy. Kierkegaard wanted to find a way to live, something worth living and dying for, something to make life significant. So there was an earnestness in his inability to get on promptly with his university studies or to find a profession to enter.

To be earnest or serious is not to be solemn. On the contrary, Kierkegaard was inspired by Socrates, and like Socrates used irony and wit against the pretensions of the academic world. He claims academia has forgotten what it is to be an actual existing human being searching for truth. For example, Kierkegaard tells us, while at university he once attended a course which was entitled, "Reality." It did not live up to its title. He says it was rather like seeing a sign in a store window saying "Suits Pressed Here," only to find, after having removed one's trousers, that the sign itself was for sale.

In his struggle for significant truth, Kierkegaard discovered that he had a "poetic talent"—not a talent for writing poetry, but for imagining possibilities. He found he could project a vast array of possible kinds of life, feel the emotions, and grasp the outlook that went with each. He did this naturally and without any strain. Kierkegaard's problem was controlling this talent; it almost drove him mad, as he had difficulty maintaining his own identity.

This poetic talent led him to reflect on the Christian way of life. At first he did not afford it any more status than he did the personalities of Faust or Don Juan. Then he began to see how distinctive a way of life it was, and how different it was from what the Christian churches around him taught and from what he saw practiced and praised as Christianity. Kierkegaard then came to the conviction that he had a vocation, a call from God, and that vocation was to produce a "literature," as he called it, a series of books each of which would describe a kind of life and a particular form of existence. In this way he would give his contemporaries an unusual picture of themselves by showing them the various kinds of life that are possible. All these ways of life are related to and contrasted to one another, and especially to the Christian way of life. As a result, Kierkegaard wrote over thirty books. Each can be read by itself, but each can be read in relation to all of the others, too, and together they sketch "existence," the way human beings can exist. He believed that within this "literature" every person would be able to find his or her own kind of life described. Each person would be able to see what he was. It would be like a mirror. Through the self-appraisal thus offered a person might become anxious to change—might desire to move to another kind of life and, ultimately, might choose to become a Christian.

This literature became one of the main sources of Existentialism, a major philosophic movement of the present century. In spite of his profound influence on this movement, it is misleading to think of Kierkegaard himself as an existentialist. Existentialism is concerned to describe how a human being may become properly human. Kierkegaard is concerned with how one may become a Christian, so he calls himself a *religious* writer, not a philosopher. He tells us that he is concerned primarily with one and only one question, How does one become a Christian?

At first sight this seems a rather minor question to spend a lifetime writing about. But his poetic talent led him to realize that there is no natural transition to religious faith by means of the intellect or the emotions. Our intellect can show us how Christianity transcends our reason. It can show us that religious faith is not an outgrowth of the human spirit, part of its essential and natural development. In short, if we have the courage and honesty to follow it, our reason can show us that we must strip ourselves free of all external and internal supports, and stand alone in our irreducible individuality, before religious truth can begin to make sense to us and eventually bring us hope and joy. Without this intensely personal pilgrimage, we cannot become Christians. We must become individuals, ready to take responsibility for what we are without any external supports or excuses before the religious life becomes a genuine possibility.

No wonder Kierkegaard found ample material for his pen!

First of all he had to describe the various kinds of life people can lead, and to show how people can wrestle free of the limitations of their ways of life so as to find their own irreducible selves. Only then could Kierkegaard begin to describe the life of religious faith, a life lived under the rule of love. So we must first examine this pilgrimage before we come to a consideration of Kierkegaard's treatment of the second of the two great commandments, Love your neighbor as yourself.

1. *The Aesthetic Life and the Ethical Life*

Now although there are many ways to live, with a multitude of variations, according to Kierkegaard, they fall into three major classes: the aesthetic, the ethical, and the religious. Each of these major types has distinctive features. Some of Kierkegaard's books treat only one of these types; for example, volume one of *Either/Or* treats only the aesthetic. Others, such as volume two of *Either/Or*, contrast the aesthetic and the ethical, and touch on the religious. Kierkegaard believes that every person falls into one of these three classes. He believes we all are *naturally* in the aesthetic; that is where we all start. Some of us leave it and move into the ethical. Some of those who enter the ethical remain there, but some eventually go on from there to the Christian life.

Let us now look at the kind of life represented by the category "aesthetic." Kierkegaard does not limit the meaning of this term to the artistic, as we do. There are dozens and dozens of ways to be an aesthete, ranging from the playboy to the scholar to the religious devoté, for there can be religious aesthetes who are not truly religious, such as those who warm themselves before the glow of some conversion experience or make a fuss over liturgy and vestments. To exhibit the variety (and yet to bring out the fundamental unity), Kierkegaard wrote several works about the aesthetic life under different pseudonyms. The author is supposed to be an aesthete rather than Kierkegaard himself, so that sometimes the convictions expressed in these books are not Kierkegaard's own. For example, volume one of *Either/Or* is a collection of essays supposedly written by different people, and they reveal different personalities—different life-styles, different ways of being an aesthete. The second volume of *Either/Or*, on the other hand, is supposedly written by an *ethical* person, a judge who addresses one of the people in the first volume. In the *Concluding Unscientific Postscript*, Kierkegaard has still another one of his creations critically review the preceding literature.

In addition, he published simultaneously with this pseudononymous material some manuscripts under his own name. At the time *Either/Or* appeared, he published under his own name two sermons called *Edifying Discourses* which do express Kierkegaard's own views. In this way he hopes to force the public to face the stark contrasts between various principal ways of life and the need to choose how to live oneself. He hopes to force people to recognize the need for becoming individuals, that is, to take personal responsibility for the lives they live by deliberately choosing them.

As I have said, there are many ways to be an aesthete but they all possess several common features, so that it is possible to describe the aesthetic life. First, it is a life based on immediacy. The aesthete takes his immediate endowments as the sole definition of the range of possibilities, without giving any thought to the possibility of another way of life beyond their range. These endowments determine the aesthete's essential identity. No choice has been made, and consequently such a person has not become an individual in spite of the enormous number of choices that he or she can make in the use of such endowments.

Second, it is a life that lacks continuity, something to hold it together, for it is forever seeking some gratification. There is a lust for enjoyment. Enjoyment is in itself innocent, but here it dominates. An aesthetic life may be crude or refined, but it moves from one thing to another and abhors the idea of commitment to any one person or thing. For then the aesthete is tied down to something which may lose its charm or interest. So it is a life made up of episodes of enjoyment; the episodes are like beads on a string, with no internal connection, and they are unable to give a life any genuine continuity. It is a life that passes from one experience to the next and lacks any cohesion between its parts.

Third, it is a life based on the accidental. If a person happens to be endowed with an exceptional talent, such as a good voice, good looks, athletic ability, or brains, and builds a life based upon any one of these, then his or her life is based on an accident. It depends on the accident of possessing one of these endowments, and it also depends on the accident of keeping it. A life based on an accident can be swept away by an accident, such as an injury in sport, or by a stroke which can reduce a genius to an idiot. Good looks fade and every voice grows old. Then a life based on any one of these is gone: *that* person, *that* identity, no longer exists.

Fourth, the aesthete judges things on the basis of their being *interesting*. The stance and attitude toward all objects, events, and people is that they either provide interest or they don't. The world is divided up into these two categories, and they are all that matters. Whether things are good or bad is irrelevant. It is only a question of, "Is it interesting to me?" The aesthete wants to be fascinated, thrilled, excited, entertained. He or she wants the extraordinary to such a degree that this need dominates a whole life.

Fifth, the aesthete is concerned with the external. There is more concern with changing the environment than with changing the self. "My troubles would be over if only I had a better job, or if my spouse were more understanding, or if I just had a bit of luck." The success of his life depends on others, on circumstances, on what happens externally. Not only is success defined by what is external, but the very identity of the aesthete is dependent on what is external.

Under a pseudonym, Kierkegaard contrasts this with the ethical life. Here the success of a life does not depend on external circumstances, but upon the person. If a person accidentally has a talent or looks and loses them, he or she can still come through. There is no need for despair; for the individual is more than his or her talent and a life built on that talent. The environment may change or it may not change; he may stay in the same job or not, but still be "successful," for an ethical person is one who fulfills obligations. An ethical person is one whose life is guided and controlled by what he conscientiously thinks to be right and good, so that success depends not on what happens outside, but on the resolve to meet obligations. Success depends on what the person does, what the person decides to do. The drama of life, its thrill, its excitement, its fascination, are not just from without but also come from within. This is the drama of self-mastery, of controlling one's desires and impulses, so that one directs one's life to meet one's obligations.

The ethical life is *significant*. Life is full of what is important because a person in doing right, in seeking good, is acting significantly. The world does not consist merely of the interesting or uninteresting, but in the good, the right, the precious, the valuable, the evil, the despicable, the dishonorable as well. The world is full of drama because the ethical person sees good and evil in conflict and acts in a significant universe, which in turn invests him or her with its own significance. Whether we live up to the good and right or not, we live in a category of significance, the category of the ethical.

Life is not a series of momentary excitements strung on a string like beads, or a series of novelties, nor is it a perpetual search for new interests. Life has continuity because it has a direction and achievements which accumulate. It grows in richness as the ethical person remains steadfast and faithful to loyalties and commitments. The passage of time is not the fleeting loss of momentary pleasures and joys. The passage of time brings with it a growing contentment with the past, as each day of faithfulness increases the riches of achievement. The ethical life grows in nobility and honor; it does not trickle away in a series of unconnected thrills and fascinating experiences. This does not mean that the ethical life does not have any thrills or fascinating experiences, but it does not consist of these, either. They are not all that matters, because what takes first place are obligations.

The aesthetic life is a life that focuses on what differentiates people, on individual differences, which mark us off from each other in talents, looks and external circumstances. It seeks out the different, the rare, the unusual, the interesting, and builds itself exclusively on these. But the ethical perceives that what is *essential* lies in what is common to people. It is a life based on what everyone can do, namely, seek to be honorable and dependable. That is something we can all aspire to regardless of the individual talents, which differentiate us and which only some have to a great degree. The aesthete bases life on and values life in terms of what distinguishes people, so that only special things and those with special things matter.

So much of life, however, is common and ordinary. So the aesthete must glamorize and idealize things in order to make life interesting, to try to invest things with blazing colors and to turn life into an adventure because the ordinary is so dull. But for the ethical person the common and ordinary are challenging. Just to be a teacher each and every day is as challenging to an ethical person as climbing Mt. Everest. To keep up one's enthusiasm, concern, and interest in the face of intractable stubbornness, indifference, a crumbling culture, and limited brains is as challenging as to strain one's muscles and exercise one's ingenuity over how to make the next leg of a climb. The adventure is not dramatic, or external, but it is a genuine adventure. It takes courage and resolve, though the achievement will rarely get into the newspaper.

This thought is captured by the well-known Scottish preacher, James S. Stewart, in one of his sermons.[5]

> I think, as one grows older, one learns to look at humanity with new eyes of wonder and of reverence: for countless are the hidden heroisms of every day. Doubtless a cynic, looking at human nature, will see only drabness and mediocrity and commonplaceness and irritating stupidity; but the man who sees only that—though he be the cleverest wit imaginable—is proclaiming himself blind and a fool.

He is missing everything. He is missing the shining gallantry and the fortitude which are everywhere in action. You cannot go through this world with your eyes open, and with some degree of sympathy in your soul, without realizing sooner or later that one of the crowning glories of the world . . . is the sheer valour with which multitudes of men and women, quite unknown to fame, are carrying themselves in the face of difficulties calculated to break their hearts.

Kierkegaard claims that the aesthetic life is one that has despair built into it. Not everyone feels the despair; it usually shows itself in the form of boredom. Boredom is the great enemy of the aesthete, and he keeps trying to push it away. This can be done by travelling for a while, trying a new hairdo, buying new clothes, changing houses, taking up yoga, enrolling for a college course, or changing marriage partners. In a myriad of ways the aesthete keeps putting off boredom by seeking variety, novelty, diversity, diversion.

Boredom is not accidental to the aesthetic life. It is built into the dynamics of a life based on gratification. Consider, for example, the section in volume one of *Either/Or* called "The Diary of a Seducer," in which you have a man who is consumed with boredom. He can no longer find any pleasure in the sensuality of sex; mere sex is a bore. It has got to be made *interesting*. So he must find a person he can idealize. Even her name must be fancy—Cordelia! Not merely Jane. He needs someone who can acquire poetic glamour. A name like Cordelia has possibilities. The seduction must be difficult to bring off. He must strive to overcome some great odds, so as to turn it into an adventure. So he invents obstacles: he will trick her into thinking that it is she who is seducing him. But the obstacle is artificially created; mere life offers him no adventures. His palate has become jaded like that of a gourmet, who needs a new taste and who finds it hard to find one. He has lived so long for gratification that life is like a desert and he is in search of an oasis. After a long struggle across the sands, how wonderful is that first drink. But he can drink in this way only once; he must then move out across the desert to get parched again before he can have the thrill of that first drink again. The interest is only in the struggle to the water. Once there, satisfaction can last only for a moment. So once the extraordinary feat of seduction is achieved, the woman loses all interest for him. He cannot even imagine a happiness or joy that is long-lasting, much less *eternal*. He has to live in a world of make-believe to produce great thrills—in his case, planning feats of extraordinary seduction to keep life interesting.

The life of this seducer is a highly individual and perverse one, illustrative of one form an aesthetic life can take. It occurs more prosaically, but just as pathetically, in academic people, who live for the next new idea, who crave novelty to keep them going, who plan extraordinarily difficult feats of scholarship to add still another volume to a library that already has over a million books. At bottom their purpose is merely to keep off the boredom which invades a life that has no significance.

Consider, too, our consuming sports mania, with thrills poured at us in game after game, event after event, all afternoon and evening. And we crave still greater ones. Announcers keep stressing how remarkable some game or performer is—but how can there be so many remarkable things going on, when they go on every week or several times a week? We have become so jaded that we need more and more claims that something is really unusual to keep us going. We are not as far advanced as were the Romans who finally had to resort to murder before their very eyes, and demanded still greater and greater spectacles of butchery because they were so bored. But we are becoming harder and harder to entertain.

Boredom is the shadow of doubt. Now doubt can occur in the realm of ideas, and such doubting has been made a virtue since the time of Descartes. Thinkers are supposed to doubt the truth of everything, to demand the credentials of everything. One is to refuse assent until the certification comes, and every proposition is scrutinized with care. Clever people can learn how to doubt just as some people can learn how to lay bricks or develop film. People can become virtuosos at critical doubting. They can doubt so much as to despair of ever knowing the truth. But the whole personality is not engaged. The person is not filled with doubt; the entire range of his or her life is not permeated with doubt. The sceptic can be very cheerful because in ordinary affairs sceptics live like everyone else, paying phone bills and eating dinner.

But there is a different kind of doubt. It is to doubt the validity of one's own life. Here the whole personality is involved. The doubt is not necessarily the result of intellectual activity, as is doubt over the truth of a theory or a statement. It is not the result of doubting the truth of, say, Marxism or Christianity. It is to doubt the validity of one's own person, of its significance, of its point. Boredom is the shadow of doubt— a doubt that can grow and grow until one despairs of one's life. One has no hope for oneself. We usually live only in the shadow, pushing off boredom. But the shadow cast by a life that lacks validity, that lacks significance, keeps coming back and the doubt grows and grows until we can come to despair.

Kierkegaard claims that the aesthetic life—the life with which we all begin—has boredom and despair built into it. For boredom is not an accidental quirk of a personality. We may keep despair at bay by fighting off boredom with ever new diversions, but the boredom keeps coming back. A person may get along fairly well if things go according to plan, if circumstances fall out right. Even so, it is hard work to keep up one's spirits and to fight off the shadow of genuine insignificance by artificial means. Some years ago the actor George Sanders killed himself in Madrid. He left behind a note in which he said that he had tried everything but that he was so bored that he could not keep going any longer.

Another way to deal with boredom and despair is to choose to become an ethical person. The aesthete has not *chosen* his or her life, for that is simply where we all begin. But it always takes a choice to become ethical, the choice whereby we determine our own identity. By choosing to recognize obligations as primary, we decide that we are to be a particular kind of person—an ethical one. We determine what is to be the basis of our life freely, and choose to give up leading a life based on the accidental, the momentary, the interesting, the agreeable, the episodic, and the external. Now obligation overrides all personal wishes. To choose the basis of one's life is to have become an individual. It is to cease to accept passively a life based on mood, whim, taste, and circumstance. It is to live in a significant world because good and evil are significant. The interesting and agreeable by themselves are but preferences, and personal preferences are not significant, although they might be unusual, interesting, and extraordinary.

To live ethically is to live in a world where time is not a burden, to be somehow filled up, and something whose passing is to be feared. We now live and act significantly in every moment of time, even the dull ones, for to be loyal and faithful is a constant condition and we actually increase our achievement with each passing day. So something of value is to be found

[66]

not just in the unusual, but also in the daily round of life. One can enjoy the sensuous, but in honorable ways; one can enjoy thrills without having the valleys of life become like Death Valley. One can enjoy the external drama, without craving it in desperation because one's inner life is so empty of all drama. The ethical life can include whatever is of value in the aesthetic life, but the aesthetic life cannot include the ethical. By its lack of restraint, in its pursuit of gratification, it finally loses the initial joys and pleasures of life.

We all like those things which give spice to life, but Kierkegaard's aesthete is one whose whole life has to be spices, in time losing not only the good that is to be found in ordinary life but also the good that is in the extraordinary as well. Kierkegaard's aesthete loses his life by seeking it. The ethical person has learned a secret about life; namely, resignation to obligations and claims is necessary in order to discover oneself. This movement to the ethical has actually to be performed. Merely to know about the aesthetic will not enable a person to escape it. You have to *become* ethical. You must resolve to live that way.

There are people who actually exemplify Kierkegaard's three types, but I expect that most of us are not sufficiently integrated to act consistently as an aesthetic, or an ethical, or a religious person. Perhaps Kierkegaard with his three types only intends to point out various tendencies in our personalities, rather than making the claim that everyone actually belongs to one of these three types. This would be enough to achieve his main purpose: to show that every person needs to make a decisive choice in order to become an individual.

The ethical life brings us to the threshold of Christianity. We cannot cross over to it from the ethical, however, without a decisive choice; for Christianity is on a different level. Pascal's three orders of body, mind, and heart is parallelled by Kierkegaard's aesthetic, ethical, and religious. What is above may include things which are below and regulate them, but what is below cannot encompass or reach what is above. To move from the aesthetic to the ethical is a move in the right direction. A person has become an individual by taking responsibility for what he or she is by a decisive choice, in recognizing the self to be under obligation. But Christianity transcends both the aesthetic and ethical levels. The nature of that transcendence can be seen easily by an examination of the principle which governs the supernatural order, namely charity, or love. Accordingly, we shall now examine Kierkegaard's *Works of Love* to see how he shows the transcendent nature of Christian love.

2. *The Christian Life*

Even after Kierkegaard drops the disguise of his pseudonyms, he continues to stress the distinctive and extraordinary nature of Christianity. He suggests it in the very title of his book on the Christian life, *Works of Love*.[6] Usually we all think of love as a way we feel, not as something that we must do. Protestant Lutherans of Kierkegaard's native Denmark and of northern Germany were also startled by the use of the word "work" because the Reformers, Luther and Calvin, so violently rejected the Roman Catholic teaching on religious works. Kierkegaard thus suggests that the Church of his day had misunderstood the Reformers. With the title of his book he calls attention to the fact that Christianity does not fit neatly into our natural way of thinking, nor even into some conventionally accepted religious ways of thinking. Instead, Christian faith is to be attained only by encountering and overcoming that which goes against the grain.

The fundamental characteristic of Christian love which marks it off from all other kinds of love is that its source is God. The love we show, if it is Christian love, has its origin in him and not in ourselves. This is all very well to say, but how can one know if it is true? Can one look into one's heart and mind, emotions and thoughts, and be able to tell whether or not the love found there has God as its source? How are we to tell whether the love which moves us is a human love or one deriving from God?

Kierkegaard deals with this question by stressing that the source of Christian love is hidden. Just as a river originates in a lake, and the lake is fed by a hidden spring, works of love originate in a reservoir of love which is fed by God. His love is a hidden source that moves, inspires, and fills us with graciousness, so that we may in turn love others. Because it is hidden we can never detect it by an examination of our thoughts and emotions, and we can always say, "But where is the source from which our actions are supposed to flow? All I can ever find when I examine myself is desires, wants, an occasional "glow," frustrations, conflicts, and that sort of thing. Self-examination never turns up the *source* of whatever love I show. If the distinctive feature of Christian love is that God is its source, show me that the love I feel has God as its source."

Kierkegaard quite disarmingly tells us that the source is hidden. Its reality cannot be discovered by self-examination. For Christian love to be known, it must first of all be believed in. One must believe in what one cannot see before one can

[69]

receive it. After one receives, one can tell from the character of the love which one has that it has come from elsewhere. One can tell that love is Christian love, even though its source is hidden, because of the fruit it bears. Human love bears human fruit; divine love bears its own fruit. Let us see how Kierkegaard develops these ideas.

Are we to say that a particular courtesy in behavior, a joyful attitude, a straightforward manner toward those socially above us, and a concern for the poor are among the characteristic fruits that derive from God? Are concern for others, warm-heartedness, and gratitude distinguishing marks of the love which has a divine rather than human source, so that we can say that these qualities are possible because of God, who is their hidden source? Perhaps they are, but perhaps they are not (WL 70–71). Kierkegaard tells us that every tree has its own fruit, but that the flower of the tree of human love and the flower of the tree of divine love at work in us very closely resemble one another. Each tree produces a blossom that at the time of blossoming—at the start of loving—can be mistaken for the other. But the fruits are different, so that as time goes on, what is earthly and what is heavenly can be distinguished. Human love is transient. "This is precisely its weakness and tragedy, whether it blossoms for an hour or for seventy years—it merely blossoms; but Christian love is eternal" (WL 25). Although Kierkegaard does not use his metaphors consistently, for human love is said to bear fruit and not just to blossom, his main point is clear: the love that comes from God bears marks of its source, the marks of eternity. Christian love is eternal; it does not change, but endures; it bears all things and never fails. So it is not to such qualities as courtesy, joyfulness, straightforwardness, and concern *as such* that we must look. All of these are no doubt good qualities, but of themselves they do not tell us where they have come from—whether from our temperament, from our upbringing, or from God. We must instead use as our standards of judgment the marks of the eternal. Then we can tell whether what we have in us is eternity present in time and space.

Accordingly, Kierkegaard points out how human love can change, indeed, change into its opposite—hatred. Hatred is a ruined love. Human love cannot bear all things. It can become jealous or possessive, so that our love changes from a great happiness to a great torment. Human love can grow notoriously weary, fade and pass away. It cannot endure all things.

But there is a love which never changes, does not pass away, but endures because its source is God. It cares for others because it is love, not because the others are distinguished by loveable characteristics. It depends on one thing only, a hidden spring.

These remarks of Kierkegaard's, though moving, are rather rhapsodical and we need some further clarification in order to distinguish a love whose source is God from human love. Kierkegaard provides further clarity by approaching the matter from a different angle, pointing out that human love which we feel is indeed that, a feeling. We do not know how it arises. It is not produced by the intellect, nor by the will, nor by calculation. It simply sweeps us marvelously (or miserably), and if it is returned, it can swell and fill us to the brim. But Christian love is a duty, an obligation, something we are commanded to do: "You shall love your neighbor as yourself" (Mt. 22:39). How in the world are we supposed to be able to do that? In the first place, even those people with whom we do fall in love, we do not love out of duty, as we have just seen. In the second place, many people are unattractive to us and there are many more toward whom we are indifferent. We can be nice to them out of a sense of duty and, perhaps even become concerned about them and willing to help them should they be in difficulty, but we don't *love* them. We love only very few of the millions of our fellow mortals and this love does not spring from a sense of duty. Yet Kierkegaard insists that in Christianity we are commanded to love our neighbors (WL 40). This then is one of the distinguishing marks of Christian love: the apparent contradiction that to love is a duty. We see here one of Kierkegaard's most frequent claims: Christianity goes against the grain and offends us with its paradoxes.

Presumably, then, if we do our duty by loving our neighbors, it is not anything human or earthly that enables us to do it. Human love is spontaneous; it wells up; it is there or it isn't. We cannot make it come. But since Christian love is a duty, something we are commanded to do, it is not the kind of love which simply arises in us willy-nilly for some people some of the time and is simply not there for others.

At this point Kierkegaard makes a very helpful use of a term he developed at the very start of his writing, the aesthetic category, which includes all that is spontaneous and immediate, all that depends on our endowment and our temperament. Love as a feeling, and as a feeling toward some and not others, belongs to the aesthetic category.

So it looks as though Christianity, because it turns love into a duty, belongs to the ethical category. It seems we are not commanded to feel, but rather to do. Hence the title of the book is not *Love*, but *Works of Love:* Christian love is something to be *performed*. So the commandment, "Love your neighbor as yourself," is apparently a contradiction only when love is considered on the aesthetic plane, as a feeling we have toward some people and not others. But the contradiction vanishes when love is seen to be a work, or an action. We are not told by Christ in the parable of the Good Samaritan how the Samaritan felt; we are told what he did.

No wonder the idea of Christian love looks strange and even offensive to those who know only human love, only an emotion stirred up by one person. Such a feeling cannot be commanded. Human love is a feeling toward only some people such as a beloved, a friend, or a child, but not toward one's "neighbor," which means toward every human being. But if the love mentioned in the commandment consists not of feelings but of actions to be performed, then such a love can be commanded.

Now, however, we encounter a new difficulty. Christian love is not just a duty, and so utterly contained by the ethical category. It also involves the *way* that actions are performed. The way that actions are carried out involves feelings and involves an emotional valence toward those whom one treats as neighbors. If there is indeed a love which is not of this world, such feelings can be commanded and can be an obligation we have toward everyone. There can be an obligation to love and to love everyone if there is a love which we can receive, a love which enables us to do what humanly we cannot do—which is to love every person.

Here is an example of this heavenly love present in human life, which is recorded by W.H. Auden.

One fine summer night in June 1933 I was sitting on a lawn after dinner with three colleagues, two women and one man. We liked each other well enough but we were certainly not intimate friends, nor had any one of us a sexual interest in another. Incidentally, we had not drunk any alcohol. We were talking casually about everyday matters when, quite suddenly and unexpectedly, something happened. I felt myself invaded by a power which, though I consented to it, was irresistible and certainly not mine. For the first time in my life I knew exactly—because, thanks to the power, I was doing it—what it means to love one's neighbor as oneself. I was also certain, though the conversation continued to be perfectly ordinary, that my three colleagues were having the same experience. (In the case of one of them, I was able later to confirm this.) My personal feelings towards them were unchanged—they were still colleagues, not intimate friends—but I felt their existence as themselves to be of infinite value and rejoiced in it.

I recalled with shame the many occasions on which I had been spiteful, snobbish, selfish, but the immediate joy was greater than the shame, for I knew that, so long as I was possessed by this spirit, it would be literally impossible for me deliberately to injure another human being. I also knew that the power would, of course, be withdrawn sooner or later and that, when it did, my greed and self-regard would return. The experience lasted at its full intensity for about two hours when we said goodnight to each other and went to bed. When I awoke the next morning, it was still present, though weaker, and it did not vanish completely for two days or so. The memory of the experience has not prevented me from making use of others, grossly and often, but it has made it much more difficult for me to deceive myself about what I am up to when I do.[7]

Kierkegaard analyzes this kind of experience by speaking of the self as consisting of body, psyche, and spirit. In erotic love the body plays an essential part. There is a sensuous attraction which is indispensable. It may involve more than that, but it cannot do without sensuous attraction and still remain erotic love. In friendship, the body or sensual appeal is not essential, for it is the psychic makeup of a person—the personality—that is essential. It is the kind of person some one is which attracts in friendship. (This attraction may be present in erotic love, too, but it is not essential to erotic love in quite the same way.) In love of neighbor all this drops away. Neither sensuous attraction or repulsion, nor the attraction of personality or culture are operative, nor any other feature which would cause us to prefer or single out one person from another. One meets others on utterly equal footing, as persons just like oneself. No one is a neighbor on the basis of physical, psychic, or cultural endowments, for a person is a neighbor on the basis of our equality before God. Such a status cannot be increased or decreased to the slightest degree by physical attributes, personality, social status, or achievements, for it is an absolute equality, an eternal equality before God.

Even though only the Good Samaritan's actions are reported, and not his feelings, the *way* he acts is revealing. He sees a neighbor in the broken wretch beside the road. He sees one with whom he has equality, an equality that cannot be destroyed by helplessness, spilt blood, or ritual differences. He was moved to act because he could see one with whom he had absolute equality, and because nothing earthly could take away eternal equality.

Auden discovered this equality by an unexpected experience, from which he learned that there is a love which is not based on personal appeal or dependent on distinctions between people. But it is not necessary to have such an experience to learn that there is such a love. The very commandment, "You shall love your neighbor as yourself," informs us that such a love exists. The aesthete finds it offensive, and dismisses it on the grounds that loving cannot be an obligation, for love is "spontaneous." It cannot be commanded. And besides, the aesthete thinks, we cannot feel love toward everyone as we feel it towards a beloved or a friend. But that very sharp collision between human love and the commandment is a sure indication that Christian love is not a human love, but is utterly distinct from it. For Christian love is an obligation we have toward every human being, and it involves our emotions, just as we saw in the experience Auden reports.

To believe in Christian love is to believe that the commandment *can* be kept. To believe in love is to believe that because God has commanded it, he will enable us to do it. To believe that obedience to the commandment is our duty, is to believe in a hidden spring of love which shall supply us. One who believes in the commandment can believe that what is not humanly possible can be accomplished. To believe in the commandment is to believe in God.

The following example from Kierkegaard will help to illustrate how Christian love does involve the emotions in our actions, so that it cannot be contained by the ethical category.

> Imagine a man who gave a banquet feast and invited to it the halt, the blind, cripples, and beggars. Now far be it from me to believe anything else about the world than that it would find this beautiful, even though eccentric. But imagine that this man who gave the feast had a friend to whom he said, 'Yesterday I gave a great feast!' Is it not true that the friend would first and foremost wonder that he had not been among those invited? But when he found out who the guests had been—now, far be it from me to believe anything else about this friend than that he would find it beautiful, even though eccentric. Yet he would won-

der and would perhaps say, 'It is a strange use of language to call such a gathering a feast: a feast—where friends are not present, a feast where the concern is not the number of servants who waited on a table.' One could call such a meal a charitable gesture, the friend would think, but not a feast. . . . [The man who had given the feast answered] 'I well perceive that our ways of using language are different, for in accordance with common language–usage the list of those invited to a feast is something like this: friends, brothers, relatives, rich neighbors—who can repay one's hospitality. But so scrupulous is Christian equality and its use of language that it demands not only that you shall feed the poor—it requires that you shall call it a feast.' (WL 90–91)

So Christian love is not only an obligation to do something rather than just to feel, but an obligation to do things in a certain way, a way that involves rejoicing. It is not "a matter of indifference under what name food is handed to the poor."

It is here that Christian love transcends the ethical category, which is concerned above all with obligations. We can have an obligation only if it is possible for us to fulfill it. If something is beyond our capacity, it cannot be an obligation. Love is a sentiment that depends on our temperament and our makeup whether we love something or someone. People differ widely in temperament and makeup. They are differently endowed. Obligations, however, are universal. They are required of everyone. Thus they must be the sort of thing everyone can do. Since the capacity to love differs widely among people, people cannot be obliged to have this or any other sentiment. Love of neighbor thus cannot be an ethical obligation.

We have seen that Christian love does not belong to the

aesthetic category because it is *universal*. That is, it is not a love for some people only. Christian love is a work, something to be done, not just experienced and a work can be commanded and performed toward any one. On the other hand, Christian love cannot be encompassed within the ethical category because there cannot be an obligation to love, an obligation not only to perform acts but to rejoice in the deed, so that it is done lovingly. The aesthetic stumbles above all on the love of *neighbor*, for it delights in love. The ethical stumbles above all on the *love* of neighbor, for it rejoices in the universal. To the aesthete Christian love demands too much, for it is to love so extensively. To the ethical person Christian love is too little; for it seems to be a mere matter of *how* one acts. Kierkegaard thus claims that the commandment breaks the bounds of both the aesthetic and the ethical categories, and that to understand the commandment properly we are forced to go to the religious category. Only so can it make sense to say that we are obliged to love our neighbor. It makes sense only if there is a love which is not human, and is able to love in spite of, not because of, distinctions between people. It makes sense only if God gives us the ability so to love; for indeed our natural endowments vary greatly, and only if all of us can hope to love our neighbors can it be an obligation for us to love our neighbors. We see once again that we must believe in a hidden spring of love for us to believe that the commandment is an obligation. We must believe that because God commanded it we shall indeed be able to love our neighbors, that God will enable us to do it. Nothing shows more clearly the divine origin of Christian love than the fact that it is commanded. The fact that it is an obligation shows that Christian love transcends human love.

We have seen in the case Auden reports that an experience

of Christian love can occur in a human being's life quite un-expectedly. It happened thus to Dante, but in his case he shows us how he put the experience to use. He tells us that as a young man he once saw a girl, known to us as Beatrice, walking down the streets of his native Florence and found himself profoundly inflamed with love. This in itself is a frequent occurrence, but in Dante's case there are two features of note. First, he tells us that he was so deeply moved that he was for the moment in a state of complete good will toward everyone. If anyone had at that moment done him an injury, he could not help but have forgiven it. Apparently more was involved than an ordinary human falling in love, for Dante not only fell in love with Beatrice, but was so filled with love that he would have been able to act lovingly toward anyone. The second feature is even more important. Dante, who found himself temporarily in a state of love and charity toward everyone, took this state to be the way he always ought to be. He accepted the obligation always to be as he had been for one moment. He accepted the obligation to love his neighbor, and had the faith that he could in a permanent way become what he had been only for an instant.

So too can we, even without such experiences, make the love of neighbor our task. We can recognize from the mere commandment itself that Christian love is a distinctive love and accept our obligation to love our neighbors.

Kierkegaard tells us that the first step in obeying the commandment is to believe it. This means that we let the commandment judge us. Jesus commended the tax-collector who could not even raise his head as he asked, "Have mercy on me, a sinner." He did not commend the Pharisee, who had obeyed the Law but was proud that he was not like others, including the tax-collector, who had failed to keep the Law. We

[79]

saw in W.H. Auden's account that the experience of love made him ashamed of the many occasions on which he had been spiteful, snobbish, and selfish. So the first encounter with Christian love, whether through an experience or through a recognition of the authority of the commandment, is an encounter with judgment. And we are being obedient when we allow ourselves to be judged. We are obedient when we hold actual enemies before our eyes again and again and confess, "This is one you have given me, O Lord, to be my neighbor." We are obedient when we call to mind and attend carefully to those we have not attended to or noticed. Our human love runs where it will; it does not run to parched land but seeks only flowery meadows. So it is also a work of love to allow the commandment to judge our self-congratulation on our kindness to those to whom we are attracted, so that we will no longer think, "Ah, how loving I am, how filled with good will I am. All this is of God." We are to attend to those words of Jesus, "For if you love those who love you, what reward have you?" What self-congratulation is due to you? "And if you salute only your brethren, what more are you doing than others?" You are going no farther than human nature allows. "You, therefore, must be perfect, as your heavenly Father is perfect" (Mt. 5:46–8). It is a work of love to let perfect love judge our self-congratulation and to recognize that those blossoms with which we deck ourselves are not of God. It is a work of love to let the commandment show that our positive relations with some people are perhaps based only upon our natural endowments, and so keep ourselves from self-congratulation.

Yet to believe in a love that judges our failures and our human love as human is also, Kierkegaard tells us, to have hope. The commandment is not only a standard of judgment but also a promise. We are told that we *shall* indeed love our neighbors. We are obliged to do what by ourselves we cannot do. We can only be so obliged because God shall make it possible by a hidden spring of love. So however downcast and discouraged we may become, we are never without hope. For God by his very commandment promises that we *shall* love our neighbor. But we can be sustained by this promise only if we recognize the commandment as an obligation. We can believe that what it commands shall be accomplished only if we acknowledge its authority over us, believe it, and so allow ourselves to be judged by it. We move from the ethical way of life into the religious by means of repentance. We find hope only by a recognition that what is required of us is beyond us, and is possible only by God's grace, possible only through a hidden spring of love.

Another task or work of love is to take the trouble to learn what Christian love is, to see its uniqueness. Christian love has many imitations, and when one of these imitations is mistaken for Christian love, then God's love is not known. Were Kierkegaard's point taken seriously, then perhaps we today might have been spared those bumper stickers which say, "Smile, God loves you." Such thoughtless phrases would be less reprehensible to Kierkegaard, however, than the spectacle of clergy speaking of love without knowing the nature of Christian love. The clergy ought to be able to speak about it clearly, if not eloquently. For Kierkegaard any laziness in the use of our intellect, which should be used with all the power and discipline that can be mustered to understand and to articulate correctly what it is that God gives us, is a serious failure in our love. We are to use our minds in order to learn and speak rightly of Christian love, so that it may shine forth clearly, and by its light judge our lives and awaken in us a hunger for the glory of that perfection which is divine love.

One common misunderstanding of the commandment concerns the phrase "as yourself." We are commanded to love our neighbors as ourselves. This is often interpreted to mean that Jesus endorses self-love. The interpretation is supported by the claim that you must in fact love yourself if you are to love your neighbor, because you are to love him as yourself. Indeed this is true; we are to have the same love for ourselves as we have for others. But this does not tell us the nature of that self-love. Is it to "feel good about ourselves," to accept ourselves as "OK"?

We discover how we are to love ourselves only when we recognize that we have a neighbor. What selfishness cannot endure is *duplication*. What the commandment asserts is that there is another who is essentially like you. To selfishness the very existence of "another" is a reproach, for it means that our endowments, our looks, our personality, our achievements, and all that distinguishes us from each other is set aside. To be placed in a class where everyone is utterly indistinguishable from everyone else is hateful to selfishness, which wants to stand out, to be noticed, to be special. The very existence of "another" is hateful because one has not loved oneself aright. To love oneself aright, that is, apart from one's endowments and personality and all that distinguishes oneself from others, is to be free of that selfishness which not only can cause one to "feel good" about oneself because of what sets one above and apart from others, but also to be free of "feeling miserable" about oneself because one has not sufficient endowments and achievements to satisfy one's desire to be even more set apart from others. To have a neighbor is to recognize *another*, a duplicate of oneself, and to have the power to rejoice in this. To

[82]

love your neighbor who duplicates you, is to know Christian love; to know Christian love is to know the right way to love yourself. As Kierkegaard puts it,

> One's neighbor is not the beloved, for whom you have a passionate preference, nor your friend, for whom you have a passionate preference. Nor is your neighbor, if you are well-educated, the well-educated person with whom you have cultural equality—for with your neighbor you have before God the equality of humanity. . . . Nor is your neighbor one who is inferior to you, that is, insofar as he is inferior, he is not your neighbor, for to love one because he is inferior to you can very easily be partiality's conde- scension and to that extent self-love. . . . Your neighbor is every man, for on the basis of distinctions he is not your neighbor. . . . He is your neighbor on the basis of equality with you before God; but this equality absolutely every man has, and he has it absolutely. (WL 72)

Here we see one of the marks of eternity which distin- guishes Christian love from all other loves: it sets aside all human distinctions and regards all people in their essential equality before God. Christian love allows all inequalities to be seen for what they are—transient, something which will pass away.

Yet Christianity is not inimical to human love. It judges it to be human but it does not condemn it. Instead, Christianity seeks to redeem human love by infusing it with that which is from above. Let us see how this can be done.

Kierkegaard rightly stresses that human love shows pref- erence. We love some people, but not others. But he also says that the very fact that we have this partiality is usually a sign of selfishness. Why does he say this? If two people are in love with each other, devoted to each other, inseparable from each other, how is this selfish?

We have such a love described by Dante in Canto 5 of the *Inferno*. In this passage Dante is visiting the second circle of Hell, where he finds the lustful. Lust is a perversion of love, and the lustful suffer a punishment which is like the actual sin they committed in life, namely, they are tossed about forever on a howling wind like the passion of lust which, because it lacks restraint, has no abiding place. In that circle Dante meets a pair of famous lovers, Francesca and Paolo, who were not promiscuous but rather great lovers, devoted to each other, entranced with each other. They are not "selfish"; their selves have disappeared in a singleminded interest in the other. Or so it seems, for the self has not really disappeared. It now *is* the other. There is a complete identification.

What is wrong with this? Selfishness has not disappeared. Each self is so identified with the other that they have absorbed each other, and find no "other"—no separate reality—in the other person. There is no person that exists apart, no person who can be a neighbor. These lovers recognize no other object in the universe; no one else exists; they are alone, cut off from all others by their passionate preference for each other. It is a passion that has no other selfishness about it apart from this: the passion recognizes no other, neither in the beloved nor anywhere else. Mutual self-absorption has taken place, so there is really only one, not two, people. Thus selfishness remains intact.

Christianity teaches self-renunciation, but when one renounces oneself what one finds is *another* and thereby indirectly one's true self that is to be loved. When such a Christian loves another with a human, erotic love, that human love does not exclude the rest of the human race. One is not cut off from others, and the obligation to love them. For when as Christians we love erotically, we love another person, one who is also a neighbor. The beloved is not absorbed in the lover, but becomes a neighbor to the lover. So humanity is preserved in the beloved by the recognition of the beloved as a neighbor, one essentially equal to the lover.

So human love—that wonderful falling in love—can be redeemed. But it is not redeemable through attempts at more and more devotion, as if the very immensity of human passion can burn out selfishness. Francesca and Paolo showed as much devotion as the immensity of passion can bestow, and yet they were not free of selfishness. Human love is redeemed by the commandment that informs us we have neighbors, and that everyone is our neighbor—even the one for whom we have a passionate preference. A person is not fulfilling the duty of Christian love by loving man or woman, child or friend, with a love that is so marvelous and intense that selfishness seems to be utterly absent. It is to love, however intensely, *another*. This kind of love is characterized by the ability and willingness to let go of the other, however painful this may be. Christian love respects the "otherness" of the beloved, his or her independence, his or her essential freedom (WL 134). This is recognized and present not only in actual cases where a separation is called for, but always, and love can bear to renounce the beloved man or woman, parent or child, or friend, because it recognizes the beloved's otherness. Christian love can bear all things and endure all things. Only thus can human love be redeemed from a possessiveness and an exclusivity which fails to recognize the existence of a neighbor in every person. All is subject to and to be submitted to love of neighbor: the erotic impulse and passion, parental love, and friendship (WL 144–7).

[85]

At the heart of every affection lies an obligation to recognize, respect, and love what is not oneself.

The tone of Dante's poetry in Canto 5 is gentle, because human love is lovely. It is not to be scorned or dismissed any more than food and drink are to be rejected in an attempt to live only from the food and drink of holy communion (WL 61). Christianity does not oppose the sensuality of human love because it is of the body. The sensuality of Paolo, Francesca, and those in the second circle of Hell is condemned because it is love that lacks the restraint and unselfishness of the love of neighbor. This is what makes the sensuality evil. But Francesca and Paolo, even in the glory of their love, are also lustful: they show no restraint, but absorb each other.

"Look well!" Virgil often says to Dante in the *Comedy* as together they visit the various levels of torment. The second of the two great commandments opens our own eyes to the exclusiveness of Francesca and Paolo's love, and makes us realize how the love of neighbor must leaven our human loves. In all our loves we need to "look well" and not neglect the second commandment, while all our loves, like all our earthly actions, need to rely on the hidden spring of divine love.

3. *The Hiddenness of God*

We have explored what Pascal calls "the order of charity," or Christian love, by a survey of Kierkegaard's account of the second of the two great commandments. Kierkegaard has shown us that our neighbors have eternal equality with us before God, and that our capacity to love ourselves and our neighbors comes from a hidden source. Crucial to this conviction is belief in God, before whom all earthly distinctions fall away. Without God we do not have equality with one another both now and forever. But how does one come to believe in God?

The only proper way to deal with this question, according to Pascal, Kierkegaard, and (as we shall see) Simone Weil, is to recognize the hiddenness of God. Failure to recognize his hiddenness leads to misguided attempts to base belief in God on philosophy or to verify Christian truth by historical evidence. Whereas a recognition of the hiddenness of God enables us to see that the only proper relationship to God is faith.

There are two major ways in which we can see that God is hidden. First, he is hidden because he is not a sense object and because he is inaccessible to the mind alone. Few would argue that God is like the physical objects which we deal with everyday. But whether God can be known by the mind alone is hotly debated. Some people have argued that from the existence and order of the world we can infer that God exists; other people have argued that we cannot. Pascal calls this deity, over whose existence people argue, the God of the philosophers as opposed to the God of Abraham, Isaac, and Jacob. Pascal believes Christianity has no stake in the God of the philosophers. The Christian God who revealed himself to Abraham, Isaac, and Jacob is inaccessible to the mind alone. One reason for Pascal's conviction is that the God of the patriarchs is the one who reveals to us our need of mercy and grace. If God were accessible to the mind alone, we would be able to know him without a knowledge of our need. So the God of mercy and grace is unknowable by the mind alone.

Even when God reveals himself, he gives only enough light to convince those who already seek him, that is, those who recognize their need for a remedy for their condition. His revelation is marked with obscurity so that those who do not seek him are unconvinced that the revelation is genuine. Until we are driven to seek enlightenment for our paradoxical nature and a remedy for our misery, God remains hidden. A change must occur in us before we are able to be enlightened by his revelation and before we may respond with faith to what is revealed.

Kierkegaard agrees with Pascal. This is why in his examination of the question, How does one become a Christian?, Kierkegaard shows that we must move from the aesthetic to the ethical and only then enter the religious life. This transition cannot be made on intellectual grounds alone, but involves our need for a satisfying life. It is only by striving to find happiness on our own terms and by the attempt to establish the validity of our lives by our achievements that we learn of our need for what is beyond us and beyond our world. Only when we are aware of our need do religious truths becoming meaningful and relevant to us. To say that God is hidden means in the first instance, then, that he is hidden from those who fail to examine themselves. This is why Pascal, Kierkegaard, and Weil concentrate so much of their attention on an analysis of human nature and the human condition.

The second major reason God is said to be hidden is because of his own nature. He is hidden not only because we fail to examine ourselves and seek him with our minds only, but because he is *essentially* hidden. This essential hiddenness is the basis of Pascal's three orders. Religious truths are on a higher level than other truths because of God's nature. They illumine our minds but they cannot be reached or verified by philosophy or history. The only way they can be affirmed is by faith.

We can better understand this by looking at Kierkegaard's treatment of the Incarnation. Kierkegaard shows why the claim that God became man is incapable of certification by history or philosophy. The only way it is genuinely faced is either when it offends us or when we respond to it with faith.

Kierkegaard explains the meaning of the Incarnation with a simple story about a king who falls in love with a humble maiden.[8] First he playfully makes fun of the childishness of romantic tales, and freely grants that we no longer live in a time when we take kings seriously. Nonetheless Kierkegaard begs his readers' indulgence because the situation contains a serious problem for a poet who wishes to write on this theme. We can see the difficulty if we imagine that we have a very unusual king, one who wishes in no way to embarrass or offend the humble maid. Should the king go to her cottage to announce his love in all his kingly glory, with magnificent garments and a large retinue, he would utterly overwhelm the girl. And besides, should the maiden manage to rise to the occasion and respond to his love, it would never be clear to the king whether it was he whom she loved or the external glory of his power and majesty. One solution to his problem might be for the king to disguise himself as a beggar and go on his own to the girl, but a new problem would then arise. Suppose that he actually succeeded in winning her love while disguised as a beggar, then she would not really love him; he is a king, but she would love a beggar. It is no good to reverse the procedure and instead of lowering the king, elevate the maiden. For this would suggest that as a humble maid she is not good enough to be loved, whereas it is precisely as humble maid that the king loves her. After exploring every feasible maneuver the poet might be driven to the only solution possible if a happy love between the king and the maiden is ever to be achieved. It is for the king actually to become a beggar, not merely to pretend, and to seek to win the maiden's love as a beggar.

This allegory, for all its apparent simplicity, shows powerfully that the Christian belief in the Incarnation is a belief that God became a man, actually *became* something which he had not been before. He was not just in the form of a man, disguised as one, but actually became one. So it is no good pointing to something which Jesus did, a miracle, for example, and saying, "Oh, that is the divine side of him showing"—as if the disguised king let his beggar's robe part slightly to show his royal vestments underneath. Nor can we point to something else, such as Jesus weeping over Jerusalem or getting angry in the Temple, and say, "Oh, that is the human side of him showing." *All* of him is human; for to perform miracles does not make a person God. And all of him, including tears and anger, is the divine one who became a man. Jesus is what God became when God became a man. Jesus is not *merely* a man; he is the man God became.

Kierkegaard claims that it is impossible for us to certify by empirical data, by its interpretation, and by reasoned argument that Jesus is divine. Historical study will not bring us as close to Jesus as were his contemporaries who saw and heard him in Palestine. But his contemporaries were no better off than we are on the fundamental and essential matter: Is Jesus God incarnate? For all they could see was a man, and indeed a humble man with no earthly greatness. His miracles—called in the New Testament "signs and wonders"—were not able to establish his divinity to the contemporary witnesses. For the working of wonders, even if genuine, could not establish that a person was God, but just that he had supernatural powers.

His signs and wonders, however, were important. They drew attention to him. They put people in tension, that is, into a situation in which they needed to decide: Is he indeed the one he claims to be or not? But the signs and wonders of themselves could not answer the question. Thus when John the Baptist was in prison, apparently troubled that the kingdom had not come, he sent his disciples to ask Jesus, " 'Are you he who is to come, or shall we look for another?' And Jesus answered them, 'Go and tell John what you hear and see: the blind receive their sight and the lame walk, lepers are cleansed and the deaf hear, and the dead are raised up, and the poor have good news preached to them' " (Mt. 11:3–5). His answer pointed to his signs and wonders. The answer to John indicates that no manifestation can be given except one which puts people into a situation in which they must make a decision for themselves. By his words and deeds Jesus forces John to decide for himself whether he is the one who fulfills the prophecies.

Thus, were we by some means transported to Palestine in the days of Jesus, we would be essentially no better off than we are now. Nothing which Jesus did or said established that he was God. His contemporaries witnessed signs and wonders that put them into a situation where they were forced to make a decision whether or not he was who he claimed to be. We do not see the signs and wonders they saw, but our situation is essentially the same. We have a *witness* or *testimony* that God became a man from those who believed him. That this is said of him by believers down the ages is firm fact, and we too must decide whether to believe what is claimed of him.

In Kierkegaard's day Hegel elevated Jesus on the grounds of his historical influence. Jesus was great because of the consequences of his life, or at least because many people believed in him and by that belief immensely influenced the course of history. So for Hegel Jesus was a world-historical figure. But this is to forget what it was like to be Jesus's contemporary, or to have lived in the days before Jesus became "historically influential." How did those people come to believe? But more importantly, great historical influence cannot show that Jesus is God. It may call attention to him and put one into a position of having to make a decision about him, but this is to be in the same position as his contemporaries who saw his signs and wonders.

Kierkegaard shows in the *Philosophical Fragments*, the *Concluding Unscientific Postscript*, and, most compellingly and simply, in *Training in Christianity* that Christianity contains an "absolute paradox." An historical person, Jesus, calls us to come to him to find peace and joy, and yet neither our sense organs nor the study of history or philosophy can certify that this historical person is to be believed. As Kierkegaard puts it so simply and well,

> The print of a foot along a path is obviously a consequence of the fact that some creature has gone that way. I may now go on to suppose erroneously that it was, for example, a bird, but on closer inspection, pursuing the track farther, I convince myself that it must have been another sort of animal. Very well. But here we are far from having an infinite qualitative alteration. But can I, by closer inspection of such a track, or by following it farther, reach at one point or another the conclusion: *ergo* it was a spirit that passed this way? A spirit leaves no trace behind it![9]

Similarly, God incarnate leaves no mark which would enable anyone to reach the conclusion that Jesus is indeed God.

One of the values of historical study is that it can remove misunderstandings about the Bible and can improve our understanding of the nature of the choice that we must make. For without historical knowledge of the time and place we would not know what a Pharisee was, nor understand why there was such a conflict between Jesus and the authorities over the Law. But this still leaves us with the question: Did Jesus indeed have authority over the Law? (because he was the divine Son?) Was he indeed the fulfillment of the Law? (because he was the divine Son?) Thus once again we see that

> there is no *direct* transition to this thing of becoming a Christian. . . . It is only by a choice that the heart is revealed (and surely it was for this cause that Christ came into the world, that the thoughts of all hearts might be revealed), by the choice of whether to believe or be offended.[10]

There is no direct move to Christianity for a person who admires and craves earthly distinctiveness and earthly joys, as does the aesthete. We are offended at being told that we must forsake the world and renounce its ability to give us happiness.

There is no direct move to Christianity for a person who has become ethical. We are offended at being told that we are not after all in possession of all that is needed to fulfill our obligations, above all our obligation to love our neighbors as ourselves, so that we cannot have repose in our own goodness.

There is no direct move to Christianity for a person who by the intellect searches empirical data, interprets history, constructs philosophic arguments. Such a person is offended at being told that Christian truth is to be held by faith.

Humility is the only proper relation to the incarnate God who comes to save: we should be humble about our immediate endowments because they cannot set us apart from others, establish our significance, and give us happiness. We should be humble because we are called to be related to all people through an essential equality. We should be humble because we can see that God incarnate is beyond the range of the intellect.

Humility is not humiliation. For a thoughtful and sincere person, faith is not blind or arbitrary; no tyranny is exercised over the intellect. What is in the heart is the experience of having tried to live aesthetically and ethically so that the invalidity of one's own person and the burden of one's inadequacy to live up to a love of neighbor are amply evident. Such a person has ample reason indeed to answer Christ's call, "Come to me, all who labor and are heavy laden, and I will give you rest" (Mt. 11:28). For Christ came into the world to reveal what is in our hearts, and the claim that he is God acts as a mirror. It shows we are of two kinds: those who take offense because they rest on their own endowments, their own goodness, their own reasoning, and those who because they find no cause for offense are blessed.

So for Pascal and Kierkegaard, God is hidden in two respects. We must examine ourselves before religious truths can become relevant and meaningful to us; otherwise he remains hidden from us. He is also essentially hidden by his very nature, so that we cannot verify religious truths by philosophy or history. It is the failure to recognize the hiddenness of God which leads to misguided attempts to base belief in God on philosophy, or to verify the truth of Christianity by historical evidence.

It is the failure to recognize the hiddenness of God which allows Christianity to be domesticated by reducing its claims to a level where they can be adjudicated by the human mind. The only way religious truth is ever genuinely faced is with faith or with offense, and any other response shows that Christianity has not been understood.

There is a further implication which we must now consider. It is because God is essentially hidden that it is so difficult to obey the first of the two great commandments. Simone Weil shows us that because God has withdrawn himself from the universe, we cannot at first love him directly, but only indirectly. Let us now turn to her account of how we are to love God, who is essentially hidden.

SIMONE WEIL

Simone Weil lived in our own century and thus shares with us an awareness of the pervasiveness of conflict and the apparent absence of God. Not only have we had two world wars, but we have come to see the presence of conflict in nature through Darwin, conflict in society through Marx, and conflict within ourselves through Freud. Simone Weil is concerned with a conflict which is as old as humanity itself: the conflict between our will and the will of God. She treats this spiritual struggle in a new and original way by connecting it to the suffering caused by nature, society, and the human psyche. Pascal and Kierkegaard had considered it only in relation to the last of these three.

Weil is more of an outsider to institutional Christianity than either Pascal or Kierkegaard. Like them, she was critical of superficial understandings of Christianity which can be found both inside and outside the Church, but unlike them she was born a Jew and was never baptized. She felt that the Roman Catholic Church, the only Christian Church with which she was well acquainted, was not sufficiently "catholic" or universal because it did not explicitly endorse what she believed to be genuine spiritual truths in some of the non-Christian religions which she had studied. Nonetheless Weil considered herself a Christian. She believed in the reality of the Trinity, in Jesus as the Incarnation of the Word of God, and in the validity of baptism and the Eucharist. She did not enjoy her self-imposed exclusion from the Catholic Church. On the contrary, she longed to receive baptism and carefully explained her situation in a series of letters to Father Perrin, a Dominican who had befriended her. These letters were published after her death in a collection called *Waiting on God*.[11]

It is primarily through suffering that she came to God. She was born in 1909, just before the First World War. Like many other French children, she gave up her ration of chocolate for the soldiers at the front and "adopted" a soldier, to whom she wrote and sent simple useful presents. Weil became very attached to her soldier, who once visited her while on leave, and his death soon afterwards made a deep impression on her.

Although she was raised in comfortable circumstances and given an excellent education, she had from early childhood a passionate identification with those who suffered, especially those who were socially inferior. During her student days Weil supported various labor organizations and spent many hours as a voluntary teacher of working men. For a short time, she took part as a volunteer in the Spanish Civil War, and later joined De Gaulle's Free French. Acutely sensitive to the suffering of others, once she burst into tears when reading about an earthquake in China. Nearly all of us are deeply moved when we witness a person's death: Weil was so sensitive that human misery, even at a great distance, could cause her to cry.

She was never in robust health and suffered all her life from severe headaches, the cause of which was never determined. She tells us that it was while she was suffering intensely from one of these headaches that "Christ himself came down and took possession of me."[12] This was in 1938. In the remaining five years of her short life, Weil reformulated in the light of the Christian faith her earlier thoughts on the human suffering inflicted by nature and society. Among other valuable writings on philosophy, history, and politics are several essays on the love of God.

Protestants tend to concentrate on teaching about God's love for us, and on our obligation to love our neighbor. But relatively little is said about our love for God, even though Jesus tells us that the first of the two great commandments is to love God. It is of course not possible completely to separate God's love for us and our love for him. ("We love, because he first loved us." 1 Jn. 4:19) Nevertheless there are few spiritual practices in Protestantism, and little theology, devoted explicitly to the cultivation of love for God. It is unlikely that this is the result solely of the rejection by the continental Reformers of the "ladder of love" so popular in medieval monastic piety, but rather that a considerable degree of spiritual maturity is necessary before God can become the object of our love. So even though love of God is the first and greatest of the commandments, we do not start there with our obedience to God. Weil is of particular interest because she shows how both religious practices and practices not presently recognized as religious contribute to our spiritual development and prepare us for loving God.

1. *The Absence of God*

Perhaps the easiest way to present Weil's thoughts on loving God is to begin with her understanding of the hiddenness of God. She shares with Pascal and Kierkegaard the conviction that God is not to be discovered through the senses, nor by those who value only material possessions and earthly power. She also shares with Pascal and Kierkegaard the conviction that God is hidden from those who value only what can be comprehended by the intellect. Whether such people accept or reject Christianity, they reduce God to the level of the mind. He is the God of the philosophers, not the God of Abraham, Isaac, and Jacob. The God of Abraham, Isaac, and Jacob, who reveals himself in the Bible, is beyond the power of the intellect to discover or to comprehend. Our entire personality, not just our intellect, must be involved in knowing him.

Kierkegaard makes explicit another conviction the other two share: God remains hidden even in his revelation. This is most evident in the case of the Incarnation. For God to become man is for him indeed to *be* a man. Thus nothing Jesus says or does, even the performance of signs and wonders, can establish that he is the divine Word incarnate. Only those who recognize their need for a savior can respond to Christ's witness with faith and devotion.

Weil emphasizes one aspect of the hiddenness of God which the other two treat only occasionally. She stresses that God is hidden by his very creation of the universe. Let us examine how the creation hides God from us, and how this relates to our love of God.

For Weil the creation of the universe by God is not a mere act of power, but also an act of renunciation. When God creates, he renounces his status as the only reality or power. He creates other realities and, in order for them to exist and to be themselves, he must pull himself back, so to speak, in order to give them room. All things exist only by God's power, and their power to operate as they do comes from him, but for them to be and to function he must allow them some degree of independence. For them to be, he must cease to be the only power there is.

The universe God has created is beautiful, but in its operations it causes immense suffering. Human beings suffer from illnesses, aging, and death. In addition to that, the freedom which God gives human beings allows them to disobey him, and a great deal of suffering and evil is caused by their actions. It is not the existence of suffering as such which causes us so much difficulty, however. The physical world involves wear and tear; plants and animals must consume something in order to live; freedom implies in turn the possibility of the abuse of freedom. Much more disturbing than the existence of suffering as such is the *distribution* of suffering. Microbes and viruses, earthquakes, floods, and the outcome of human actions do not distinguish between those who stand in their paths. If those people who disobey God suffered or suffered more as a consequence of their disobedience, it would make sense. But what we find is that both those who seek to obey God and those who disobey him are equally vulnerable to suffering and equally liable to prosper. The operations of the natural world and the consequences of human actions do not punish and reward people according to whether they obey or disobey God. It is this anomaly which so deeply troubled the people of Israel in the Old Testament, and which found its most complete expression in Job and the Psalms: "It is all one; therefore I say, he destroys both the blameless and the wicked" (Job 9:22). Jesus points to the same indifference when he says of God, "He makes his sun rise on the evil and on the good, and sends rain on the just and on the unjust" (Mt. 5:45).

Weil connects this fact to the commandment that we are to love God. For her, force is the opposite of goodness. Force compels; goodness attracts. To use force can mean not only a literal use of physical compulsion, but also to make something without freedom, such as a machine which operates as it does because of the way its mechanism is designed. All nature obeys God because of the way he has designed it. Nature is a realm in which each thing acts as it does because it cannot act in any other way. God in creating it has given it independence. But although independent, it operates as it does according to the character he has given to it, and so it acts according to God's will by compulsion.

God desires that we obey him, but not under compulsion. He might, however, have sought to gain our obedience indirectly. He could have used nature and the course of human actions to punish and reward us. Should we obey him, we would receive earthly rewards; should we disobey him, we would receive earthly punishments. But then we would obey him, if we were sensible, because he satisfies our earthly desires. We would obey him as a *means* to our ends. We would not love him with all our heart, soul, strength, and mind. He would not be the good to which we were utterly devoted. We would be devoted to the earthly goods which obedience to him makes available to us.

It is because God wishes our relationship to him to be one of love that he hides himself. That is, he creates and orders the universe and disposes of human affairs in such a way that we may freely come to love him, and to find in him rather than in the creation, our highest good.

But let us step back for a moment from Weil's account of God's withdrawal from his creation, and consider only our own attitude toward nature. Our attitude toward the physical universe is ambivalent. We find the universe beautiful and much in it that is good. But we know that it is dangerous. We attempt to control it as much as we can, but our control is limited. The universe's indifference to our concerns, values, and moral qualities causes us not only to fear it, but also to be repelled by it. We find it alien because it pays no heed to us; nor does it have any regard for us as human beings. It treats us no differently than it does any other natural object, operating according to its own built-in necessity and enclosing us in its operations for good or for ill. Its indifference keeps us from being attracted to it as something which is utterly good. If we believe in God, we are tempted to rail against God because of nature's indifference. And it is precisely because of nature's indifference that many people say that there is no God.

Nature thus stands as a barrier between us and God. Were nature such that we found it thoroughly and utterly good, rather than indifferent, we would find it very plausible to believe that its source (should it have one) is similarly good, and loves us. But nature is not thoroughly and utterly good from our point of view. For us to find it credible that its source is good, and that its alleged creator loves us, we must overcome the barrier caused by nature's indifference toward us. Only if we can find the creator, and find him to be good, can we believe that he has interposed an indifferent universe between himself and us in order to win our devotion to the good that he is, rather than to the good things he provides for us through his creation.

Weil tells us that although the created universe is a barrier between us and God, it is also a means whereby we may reach him. "This world is a closed door. It is a barrier, and at the same time it is a passage."[13] It is by honestly facing the barrier formed by the universe that human beings can make an opening in themselves so God may enter into them. It is because God is present in ourselves that we can have the kind of love which does not seek earthly rewards, but is a love for him who is beyond all earthly good. With such a love we can then love God's hidden presence elsewhere in the universe. For although God has limited the exercise of his power, his purity is present in the created universe. He is "secretly" present—that is, present in purity, not in power—in our neighbors, in nature, and in religious rites. Let me expand on these difficult matters, first showing how the universe by being a barrier can at the same time be a passage, by which God's love can enter us.

For Weil the universe consists of several levels. At the bottom there is simply space. On the next level is matter, which compared to space is extremely small. For example, it takes light, which travels 186,000 miles per second, four and one-half years to reach the earth from the nearest star, and two million years to reach us from the nearest galaxy. The next level is living matter, which is only a small fraction of all matter. The diameter of our planet is approximately nine thousand miles, but life is found only on its surface and a few miles above and below it. Among living things, we have the highest level of intelligence, and the overwhelming majority of our thoughts are egocentric. We tend to see, feel, and understand everything from our own point of view. Occasionally we escape to some degree from our egocentricity and perceive things as they really are, free of the distorting effect of our wishes, interests, fears, and self-importance. We then experience how small we are compared to the vastness of the universe, and the vastness of its indifference toward us.

Pascal, as we have seen, juxtaposes our insignificance to our greatness to show that our nature is paradoxical. But Weil believes that the experience of our insignificance is itself of considerable spiritual importance. The experience of perceiving the universe as it is, free of the distortions caused by our ego-centricity, gives us the possibility of finding a good that is beyond it. According to Weil, it is the absence of God which gives us the desire for his presence.

Weil says that we do not begin to become religious by beginning to search for God, because God is utterly unrepresentable to our senses. At first we seek only for those things which we can imagine or that we can picture to our senses and minds. We have a *need* for God, but not a *desire* for him. That need has the possibility of becoming a desire when we discover that the universe has no good, no goal, no purpose, but that it is indifferent to us.

The experience of nature's indifference as valid experience is supported by the findings of modern science. One of its achievements is the discovery that human concerns and values are not present in nature. In the ancient Greek world nature was thought to support human goals and values. This idea was reformulated by the medieval scholastics and it dominated Western culture well into the seventeenth century, when it was set aside by modern science as irrelevant for understanding the way the natural world works. Human beings, who act according to purposes, exist in a universe which operates by causes only and has no purposes. It is thus utterly indifferent to our pursuits.

Although modern science views the universe this way, we easily overlook the spiritual value of this outlook. As long as we can employ the sciences to achieve human purposes, we can ignore the fact that the universe unveiled to us by science is one which is utterly indifferent to human well-being. No goal for human life is ever revealed by science; no finality is uncovered as the end of our quest for fullness. Even those who stress the intellectual satisfaction resulting from scientific study as an end in itself, neglect the fact that intellectual satisfaction is only one aspect of human life and does not give us all that we need. In such ways as these the spiritual significance of the indifference of the universe is overlooked.

The indifference of the universe can become spiritually significant only if we honestly face the fact that the pleasant and good things of this world are not sufficient to satisfy us. As Weil puts it,

> We are well aware that the good which we possess at present, in the form of wealth, power, consideration, friends, the love of those we love, the well-being of those we love, and so on, is not sufficient; yet we believe that on the day we get a little more we shall be satisfied. We believe this because we lie to ourselves. If we really reflect for a moment we know it is false. . . . We have only to imagine all our desires satisfied; after a time we should become discontented. We should want something else and we should be miserable through not knowing what to want.
>
> A thing that everyone can do is to keep his attention fixed upon this truth.[14]

If we hold firmly to the uncomfortable truth that there is nothing in this world which can fully satisfy us, the indifference of the universe, far from being a barrier, becomes a passage. For the operations of nature and the course of human affairs, even if favorable, cannot give us a good whose possession would end our desire for something else or something more.

The indifference of nature and the course of human affairs, if we have any awareness of the world's inability to satisfy us, causes us to develop a degree of detachment from the world. The more we reflect on its indifference, the more detached we become. To have a degree of detachment from the world creates an opening in us for God to enter.

God does not come to us in power and glory, but, as Weil puts it, secretly. He is not visible to the senses, and at first he does not make his presence known in any way. Instead he plants a seed in us. In time the seed grows, and when it becomes sufficiently large, we find ourselves with a *desire* or a love for God.

According to Weil, our love for God is actually the result of God's presence in us. The seed is his Spirit, or his love, in us. Our only involvement is the recognition that the universe is indifferent and is unable to give us fulfillment. This momentary recognition, however, is not enough. For we must allow this recognition to become a permanent part of our outlook and to affect our entire personality. Otherwise, even should God plant his seed, it is expelled by our return to the pursuit of earthly good and a concern for the mere utility of the sciences for our purposes. We must retain the recognition that this universe, for all its immensity and variety, is limited; it is unable to give us fulfillment. Only thus is there room for the seed to remain and not be expelled; only thus is there time for it to grow.

This recognition of nature's indifference is difficult to sustain because at first all we experience is the futility and the pointlessness of life. Since the seed is small and is put into us "secretly," we are not at first aware of its presence. We do not have any particular sensation or any religious experience. It is only after the seed has grown that we begin to love.

[107]

2. *The First Form of Implicit Love*

Weil's view of the hiddenness of God results in a distinction between the implicit and the explicit love of God. By creating a universe, God limits himself. The physical universe is allowed to operate according to its given nature. He does not interfere with it in such a way as to render its operations beneficial only to the pious and injurious only to the impious. In addition, human freedom results in sin and evil. Pious as well as impious people are exposed to the suffering which results from human actions. God limits himself in order to win our devotion to himself, and not to have us obey him merely because nature and human affairs are so ordered as to be always beneficial to us, or always beneficial only to those who obey him. Although God has limited the exercise of his power, and in that sense is said to have withdrawn himself from the universe, he nonetheless is present in it. He is "secretly" present in our neighbors, in nature's order and beauty, and in religious practices. By loving these, we indirectly or implicitly love God. We love things which are not God, but because God is present in them, we are also implicitly loving him. Our initial obedience to the first commandment which enjoins us to love God is thus at first obeyed by a love of these other things.

We say God is present in them secretly because his power or rule is not manifest in the world, since he has withdrawn it; he is instead present only in purity or holiness. Because he is present in his creation we can love him, even though at first we do not realize that it is he whom we love. We love our neighbors, nature's order and beauty, and religious practices for their own sakes, but our love for them prepares us for an

explicit love of God. We can through a long process of purifi-
cation come to obey the first commandment by loving God
explicitly, or directly. God can thus become the object of our
love, even though what we are in contact with in our daily life
are people and the operations of nature. His presence in them,
and in religious ceremonies, gives us access. We shall now
examine each of the three forms of implicit love of God and
show how they enable us to develop an explicit love of God.

We have come to consider the first commandment after
our examination of the second, because it is by loving our neighbor that we have access to God and so begin to obey the first
commandment. But the two commandments are two and not
one. When we love our neighbor, our neighbor is the object of
our love. But God's presence in our neighbor means that he,
too, is the object of our love. This is clearly stated in a parable
of Jesus.

> Then the King will say to those at his right hand, "Come,
> O blessed of my Father, inherit the kingdom prepared for
> you from the foundation of the world; for I was hungry
> and you gave me food, I was thirsty and you gave me
> drink, I was a stranger and you welcomed me, I was naked
> and you clothed me, I was sick and you visited me, I was
> in prison and you came to me." Then the righteous will
> answer him, "Lord when did we see thee hungry and feed
> thee, or thirsty and give thee drink? And when did we see
> thee a stranger and welcome thee, or naked and clothe
> thee? And when did we see thee sick or in prison and visit
> thee?" And the King will answer them, "Truly, I say to
> you, as you did it to one of the least of these my brethren,
> you did it to me." (Mt. 25:34–40)

This parable teaches that although we do not realize it at the time, when we love our neighbor we are also loving God. It further suggests that an implicit love becomes an explicit love when we become aware of God himself as the object of our love.

The distinction between an implicit and explicit love of God enables us to see that at first we love God by loving other things, including our neighbors, and only when such a love has reached a high degree of purity, do we love God explicitly. So the commandment to love God is a distinct commandment even though at first we obey it only through obeying the second commandment.

In his treatment of the love of neighbor, Kierkegaard emphasized the absolute equality each of us has before God. Simone Weil fully agrees, and in her discussion of it, she concentrates on situations of inequality and shows how love creates a balance.

She contrasts two uses of power, one which imposes itself by force and another which respects others. She cites a passage from the ancient Greek historian Thucydides to illustrate the contrast. Thucydides in his *History of the Peloponnesian War* describes how the Athenians, who were at war with Sparta, wanted to force the inhabitants of the little island of Melos, who were neutral, to join with them. The inhabitants, when faced with an ultimatum either to join the Athenians or to be destroyed, appealed to justice, claiming that the Athenians had no right to violate their neutrality. The Athenians did not even try to prove that their demand was just. They pointed out that when human beings have a dispute to settle and neither has the power to impose a solution, then they have to consider what is fair in order to come to an understanding. But when we are able to get our own way because we are much stronger than our adversary, then justice can be ignored because the stronger can compel the weaker to give way. When the islanders still refused to join them, the Athenians razed their city to the ground, put all their men to death, and sold all their women and children as slaves.

To love our neighbors as ourselves is to consult justice whenever there is a matter to be settled between us. We are to do this not only in instances where there is more or less equal strength, but also when there is significant inequality. It is love which enables us to treat those who are not equal as equal. It is respect for the reality of others as people which enables us to treat others as equals even though they do not have as much strength, social prestige, or wealth. One use of power, then, is to employ it to the fullest to get what we want. Another is to restrain ourselves in our use of power out of respect for others.

Love of neighbor not only causes us to act as though others are equal, it also actually makes us equal. It is not easy to speak courteously to people who are socially inferior, to pay attention to their point of view, and to reach a just solution in a dispute with them. But it is harder still to do these things without feeling a sense of superiority because we have done them. If we do feel superior, then we have not loved our neighbors; love does not feel superior.

Perhaps the way love of neighbor actually makes us equal can be seen in this way. All people, however lowly they may be, are still people, and love of neighbor is a recognition of this essential equality. It is not possible to show respect towards others and then to believe we are superior to them because we have shown them consideration when we did not have to. For it makes sense to say of someone, "I didn't have to take so much trouble over him because he is poor, uneducated, and unattractive." But it does not make sense to say of a person who is poor, uneducated, and unattractive, "I didn't have to take so much trouble over him because he is a person."

To love our neighbors requires us to detach ourselves from thinking that our essential identity is formed by the presence or absence of talent, achievement, and social position. To be able to renounce all that distinguishes us as being higher or lower than others is extremely difficult. Weil thinks that

> to make that effort is an approach, not towards suffering but towards death; and towards that death which is more radical than that of the body and equally repellent to nature: the death of the thing within us that says, 'I.'[15]

What looks like death is actually what leads to a resurrection, she says, but at the time of renunciation this cannot be foreseen. The idea of loving our neighbor, regarded with utmost seriousness and without compromise, only enables us to foresee that "death." We can grant that we often fail to be thoughtful and kind, and we admit our need to improve. But we find it nearly impossible to embrace our obligation to be perfect, to love our neighbors as ourselves, because we are repelled by the totality of self-renunciation that it requires.

It is only our firm adherence to the fact that there is nothing in the world which would fully satisfy us that gives us some degree of detachment from all the earthly things that create distinctions between human beings. That degree of detachment gives the seed of love planted in us by God room to grow. It is the love of God in us, and not our own goodness, that goes out to others. Because it is not by our own goodness that we love our neighbors, we can show concern and consideration for others, both high and low, without a sense of self-congratulation or pride for having done so.

Mary, Jesus' mother, is a paradigm of the way love of neighbor is actually God's love and yet is at the same time an action which we must perform. Mary bore the Word of God in her womb. He was from above, not the fruit of any human action. By her consent to bear what was from above, Mary bore a child which was *her* child. Such is the love we have for our neighbor, and indeed such are the other forms of implicit love of God which we may have. Love derives from the seed God has planted in us. Because of our steadfast adherence to the fact that the world cannot satisfy us, the seed has room and time to grow. When it begins to manifest itself in action, we yield our will to it. By this consent to that love at work in us, by our acceptance of it, it becomes ours. Because we consent, it is we who love with a love that comes from God.

The love of neighbor prepares us for an *explicit* love of God. For as we increase our ability to see ourselves and others quite apart from the identity given to us by earthly circumstances, we are progressively made free to love without hope of any earthly reward. This means we are better able to love God himself who is beyond all earthly goods, and to love him in spite of our earthly circumstances.

Let us now look at those who are poor, or socially inferior in other respects, and see how according to Weil they may love their neighbors. People who receive benefits from others may love their neighbors by means of their gratitude. When those of us who give and those who receive both adhere to our essential equality, then it is possible to receive with our self-respect remaining intact. We can recognize that the consideration we are shown and the trouble taken for us is more than is necessary, given our inferior position. This can occur if the sole object of our attention is the generosity we have been shown. It is natural for those who are inferior to envy those who are above them; the latter gain an imaginary elevation. But if we recognize that we are all essentially equal, what we attend to is not the higher status of our benefactors, but their generosity. Were the position of those who recognize our essential equality reversed so that those who were superior were now inferior, and vice versa, their relationship would still be one of generosity and gratitude.

If, on the other hand, people who are inferior are not shown consideration as people, they can still love their neighbors. They can recognize that no one acts out of love for the neighbor except by a love which is from above. They thus can be free of hatred for those who do not treat them as people. They can pray for those who scorn them, and look on them with pity.

Weil was devoted to social reform all her life. She believed that attempts to overcome social injustice can be free of unrestrained hatred for those who are privileged and those who are oppressors, and that there can be concern for their good. But social reform whose sole or primary motivation is envy of those who have power could not, she believed, give rise to social justice. We cannot here go into her social philosophy, which is contained in the two books *Oppression and Liberty* and *The Need for Roots*. The key to a true liberation of the oppressed, she believes, is found in the parable of the Good Samaritan, which was told by Jesus to explain what it is to love our neighbor. Weil interprets it as a desire to restore a person who has been dehumanized to the status of a person, one who

> is only a little piece of flesh, naked, inert and bleeding beside a ditch; he is nameless, no one knows anything

about him. Those who pass by this thing scarcely notice it, and a few minutes afterwards do not even know that they saw it. Only one stops and turns his attention towards it. The actions that follow are just the automatic effect of this moment of attention. The attention is creative. But at that moment when it is engaged it is a renunciation. This is true, at least, if it is pure. The man accepts being diminished by concentrating on an expenditure of energy, which will not extend his own power but will only give existence to a being other than himself, who will exist independently of him. (WG 103)

Revolutions may topple an unjust social order. But there is no genuine hope unless the "liberators" now exercising power desire that others may exist independently of themselves. This requires self-renunciation rather than self-glorification, and resistance as well to the temptation to impose a prescribed order on others. Weil's fundamental conviction concerning the love of neighbor is that God seeks to enter us so that his love causes us always to consult justice in all our relations with each other, even when we do not have to.

3. The Second Form of Implicit Love

The second form of the implicit love of God is the love of the order and beauty of the universe. It too involves renunciation. When loving our neighbor, we renounce the unrestricted use of our power for the sake of other people; when loving the universe, we renounce the illusion that we are its center.

> Each man imagines he is situated in the centre of the world. The illusion of perspective places him at the centre of space; an illusion of the same kind falsifies his idea of time; and yet another kindred illusion arranges the whole hierarchy of values around him. This illusion is extended even to our sense of existence, on account of the intimate connection between our sense of value and our sense of being; being seems to us less and less concentrated the further it is removed from us. (WG 114)

We have already seen how it is possible for us momentarily to be free of this illusion. When we become aware of how small we are compared to the immense size of the universe, we sometimes recognize for a moment how utterly independent of us it is. Its indifference is especially brought home by the suffering it causes. Benefits and harm come to people indiscriminately, and do not fit our patterns of justice or fairness. No allowance is made for our sense of values. Its indifference can also be brought home to us by a recognition that there is no good in the universe which can give us complete satisfaction. We find it difficult to make this fact part of our basic outlook, because the only way to do so is by getting rid of our sense of self-importance.

> All men know this, and more than once in their lives they recognize it for a moment, but then they immediately begin deceiving themselves again so as not to know it any longer, because they feel that if they knew it they could not go on

living. And their feeling is true, for that knowledge kills, but it inflicts a death which leads to a resurrection. But they do not know that beforehand; all they foresee is death; they must either choose truth and death or falsehood and life.[16]

As we saw earlier, such renunciation creates an opening in us for the seed of divine love to enter us in secret. But we do not face the independence and indifference of the universe for the purpose of receiving such a seed. We face it and accept it, if we accept it at all, simply because it is true.

Even though nature is indifferent, we find it beautiful. At every magnification a leaf looks beautiful; from every distance in space, the earth is radiantly beautiful. Of course the beauty we see is a result of the interaction of light rays reflecting off objects and our sense organs. But this makes the prevalence of sensuous beauty all the more remarkable, as it is of no use in the evolution of our species and of no use beyond its enjoyment. Not only is the universe sensuously beautiful, but its order delights our minds. Many scientists have commented on the joy and understanding that nature's order gives them. We thus find it easy to love the universe with our senses and intellect. It is when the operations of the universe run counter to our plans or when they injure us that we find it unloveable. We are attracted to it when it confers benefits, but it repels us when it injures us. But the same laws which make it sensuously and intellectually beautiful cause it at times to run counter to our wishes. We can nonetheless love the world in adverse circumstances, not finding it loveable but consenting to its indifference toward us, so that we accept our subjection to its power. This is only possible because we have faced the indifference of nature and made acceptance of it a part of our outlook. We have consented to God's renunciation of his power to rule nature. We can believe that we are placed at a distance from God, with an indifferent universe between us, so that we may come to love him. Evil and suffering, which result from human freedom as well as the indifference of nature, are the price God pays to win our devotion to him. He withholds his rule over nature and human affairs so that piety and impiety do not receive earthly rewards and earthly punishment in such a way as to compel us to obey him.

So the distance between us and God caused by the created universe, in both its physical and social aspects, is a measure of his love. To consent to this arrangement is to love God. To love the universe, with its suffering and evil, is not to love suffering and evil. They are but the signs of the distance between us and God. This distance can be loved as it was created by love.

We are to seek to relieve distress and to remove its causes, whether natural or human, as much as possible. What we are to believe is that distress and evil are permitted to occur only because God, out of love, restricts himself. We are to consent to such an arrangement, even when we find it causes us and others to suffer.

When we seek to restore those who are reduced to mere "things" by the operation of nature or by human action, our love resembles God's creative love. He created human beings with the ability to give or to withhold their assent; we by our love seek to restore to them that status. When we renounce the illusion that we are at the center of the universe, our renunciation is similar to God's own at creation. He divested himself of his power to rule the universe; we divest ourselves of our false divinity. He desires that our love be like his love.

Although God withholds his power, he is present in the

universe. The order of the world is created by the Logos, a word that has a large range of related meanings. Usually when it occurs in the New Testament, "logos" is translated as "word." But "logos" also means ratio or proportion, and hence order, and it is this particular meaning which Weil develops. She regards the order of the world as a *ratio* of forces which are so proportioned as to result in an ordered universe. This ratio, or "logos," is the Logos, the Word of God spoken of in the opening of John's gospel. Thus for Weil the second person of the Trinity is present as the principle of the world's order. The beauty of the universe which results from this order (in relation to our sense organs and intellect) is the beauty of the Logos. We thus have contact with God through the order of the universe when we perceive its beauty through our senses and our minds, and also through our bodies when it blesses us or injures us.

The operations of nature are particularly important to Weil's concept of the spiritual life. For example, sensuous beauty, which results from nature's order, nourishes or feeds the seed of love in us. Beauty is heavenly or divine food. With the nourishment it gives, we grow in love not only for the world but also for our neighbors. Beauty nourishes the seed of love and also helps us to make more room for its growth. The beauty of the universe attracts and holds our attention as though it were about to give us something of immense value. We gaze at it, waiting in expectation for some good which we cannot name, but which we sense would give us completeness. It thus increases our longing for a good which would give us lasting satisfaction. This increases our detachment from earthly goods; we are able more and more to see these as indeed good, but nonetheless limited and so unable to give us the fullness for which we long. In this sense, beauty has a purifying effect on us.

Now we are able to get an idea of how our love of neighbor and our love of the universe are a preparation for the explicit love of God. To love God is to look to him as our ultimate good, indeed, as the only good which can satisfy us or give us fulfillment. But he cannot be represented to our senses nor pictured to our imagination. Thus we seek to find fullness or happiness from the things of this world instead. The world does not contain our ultimate good, but as we have seen we can resist facing this.

Whatever helps us to overcome this resistance and free us from the delusion that earthly goods are the ultimate good, enables us to attend to God. For it is detachment from the things that create distinctions between us that enables the love planted in us to grow, so we may go forth loving our neighbor and loving the universe. Since God is secretly present in both, we have contact with him in loving them.

Our love for our neighbors is far from perfect, since we find it hard to disregard looks, talents, achievements, and social position as being an essential part of their identity. We find it difficult to accept the indifference of nature and to consent to the suffering it causes. We improve in our love of neighbor and the universe as we develop more and more detachment from earthly goods as our ultimate good. It is not that we love people less, or that we become indifferent to suffering. On the contrary, our gratitude for the love others show us and our compassion for those who suffer are heightened by our detachment. Our increasing freedom enables us better to renounce ourselves so we can attend to our neighbors and love the universe in spite of the injury it inflicts on us. When our love of neighbor and our love of the universe have reached a high degree of purity by their detachment from earthly goods, God comes to the soul. The good that he is fills it and gives it felicity. Now we love him explicitly, or directly.

He does not come as a reward to those who have loved their neighbors and the universe. But the effect of loving them better and better is to turn us with increasing attentiveness to where God dwells, though he dwells there in secret. All that is needed for God to come to the soul is attentiveness to the places where he is—in our neighbor, in the universe, and, as we shall see, in religious ceremonies.

Weil does not like the expression "seeking God" because at first God is present to us only secretly. She writes,

> How could we search for God, since he is above, in a dimension not open to us? We can only advance horizontally; and if we advance in this way, seeking our good, and the search succeeds, this result will be illusory and what we have found will not be God.[17]

It is only because God is present here below in our neighbors, in nature, and in religious ceremonies that we can reach him. But since he is present in them secretly, we cannot seek God. It is only by attention to what is not God that we eventually have contact with him, a contact which becomes direct or explicit; we experience the unique good that God is only after the long preparation of implicit love.

The French government issued a postage stamp to honor Simone Weil. Underneath her picture are these words. "Attention is the only faculty of the soul which gives us access to God." This expressed the core of her understanding of the spiritual life.

The highest form of love of which we are capable in this

life, however, is not an explicit love of God. When we love God explicitly, we experience the joy of God's goodness. For Weil, the paradigm of perfect love is the love Jesus shows on the Cross. He dies as a criminal, condemned by both the civil and religious courts, ridiculed and scorned. Not only are all earthly goods taken away, but even the awareness of God's love. He cries out, "My God, my God, why hast thou forsaken me?" Nonetheless, Jesus continues to love the Father and to trust him, and this love is perfect. For Jesus continues to love the Father without the presence of any *good* to love: neither an earthly good nor the good that is the Father. Only those who are afflicted, as was Jesus, have the opportunity to love God perfectly in this life. This is not a love we are to try to achieve. Affliction is not to be sought, nor does Weil believe that it can be sought, as it is so horrible that everything in us seeks to escape it. But we are to prepare ourselves for the possibility of affliction, since it may happen to anyone, and when it strikes those who are unprepared for it, it crushes them completely. The implicit love of God can prepare us to endure affliction, even if we have not experienced God's presence explicitly at any time.

4. The Third Form of Implicit Love

The third form of the implicit love of God is the love of religious practices. Unlike the love of neighbor and the love of the universe, whereby people may love without having God in mind, love of religious practices necessarily involves thinking about God. Weil insists, nonetheless, that the love of religious practices is an implicit love of God because there is no immediate contact with him. God is present in our neighbors and in the beauty and order of the universe just as much as in religious practices, and in the same way.[18]

It is important that God is present in these other two spheres because all religions are not equally suitable for calling on the name of God, and the religion most people practice is the religion of their country or the circle in which they are brought up (WG 136–7). Besides, many people, owing to various circumstances, are repelled by institutional religion. Still, religious rites, although not absolutely essential, are an important way for people to have contact with God. Their particular value is that they give us tangible contact with what is perfectly pure, and, as we will see, what is pure can take away evil. People are not perfectly pure, even though God is secretly present in them. Nothing in the created realm is perfectly pure except the beauty of the universe taken as a whole. The beauty of the universe, however, cannot be contained in anything tangible. Religious rites are both perfectly pure and tangible.

> This is not on account of their own particular character. The church may be ugly, the singing out of tune, the priest corrupt and the faithful unattentive. In a sense this is of no importance. It is as with a geometrician who draws a figure to illustrate a proof. If the lines are not straight and the circles are not round it is of no importance. Religious things are pure by right, theoretically, hypothetically, by convention. Therefore, their purity is unconditioned. No stain can sully it. . . . This purity is unconditional and perfect, and at the same time real. (WG 140)

Such a claim cannot be demonstrated by argument, Weil notes, but only believed because of the effect of religious things on us. For if we attend to them, they have the power to remove our evil.

Her conviction that Christ is present in the Eucharist is not the claim that bread ceases to be bread and wine, wine. There is no explanation of how he is present there or in other religious rites and practices. "His presence in the Eucharist is truly secret since no part of our thought can reach the secret" (WG 141). In this respect Weil is closer to the tradition of the Reformed Church than the classical Roman Catholic position of transubstantiation. The incomprehensibility of Christ's presence in the Eucharist and other religious rites does not make a greater demand on our reason, she claims, than the applicability of pure mathematics to our world.

> No one dreams of being surprised that reasoning worked out from perfect lines and perfect circles which do not [materially] exist should be effectively applied to engineering. Yet that is incomprehensible. The reality of the divine presence in the Eucharist is more marvelous but not more incomprehensible. (WG 141)

According to Weil, it is by our paying attention to where God is that we have contact with him. But we can only fix our full attention, she claims, on something tangible, and we sometimes need to fix our attention on what is perfectly pure. Only this act destroys part of the evil that is in us. It is the perfect purity of Christ present in the Eucharist that takes away sin.

We see here that Weil is primarily concerned with the process of sanctification in her discussion of the forms of the implicit love of God. In theology there is a distinction between justification and sanctification. We are justified, that is, forgiven and saved from damnation, by the love of God. As Paul expresses it, "While we were yet sinners, Christ died for us" (Rom. 5:8). We are counted righteous before God because of Christ. This is the good news.

We are called to respond to the gracious love of God shown to us in Christ, and such a response involves yielding ourselves to God. This is the process of sanctification in which all that holds us back from yielding ourselves is progressively removed and the seal of love for God is allowed to grow more and more until we love him with all our heart and all our soul, all our strength and all our mind. It is called sanctification from the Latin term "sanctus," meaning "holy," or that which is divine. Our task is then to love God with a love which is from above, and which grows until all our being is directed by that love. We are then perfectly obedient, loving him and our neighbors as we ought. Kierkegaard is referring to the process of sanctification when he says that no one *is* a Christian; we are all *becoming* Christians.

What is the process by which perfect purity destroys evil? Let us approach it by recalling Pascal's expression, "the misery of man without God." To be without God, separated from him, is to be in a state of sin; to be in this condition is to experience misery. Pascal, Kierkegaard, and Weil analyze in detail our boredom and anxiety, and describe the ways we seek to overcome them with activities, possessions, achievements, and dreams of a better future. Perhaps we can capture the essence of their point by one of Freud's remarks. He once said that the aim of psychoanalysis is to relieve people of their neurotic unhappiness so that they can be normally unhappy.

Weil claims that sin and the misery we feel are united in us, and that their union is evil. The power of evil over us is not just that we do evil things and fail to do good ones, but it is our inability to remove it by making improvements in our personality and character. For it is not this or that aspect of our characters that is our fundamental difficulty. It is we ourselves; we are evil. This ugliness we cannot bear. Thus we project it onto others and onto our surroundings. We see evil in other people and in our surroundings. As Jesus expresses it, "Why do you see the speck that is in your brother's eye, but do not notice the log that is in your own eye?" (Mt. 7:3).

People and other things around us are not perfectly pure, so that the evil we see is frequently there, even if we tend to exaggerate its magnitude. So when we condemn the evil we see and do so because we are evil, the evil that we are is simply reflected back. But that which is perfectly pure, because it has no evil for us to condemn, does not reflect our evil back. It absorbs it. Thus Jesus says, "Blessed is he who takes no offense at me" (Mt. 11:6).

As evil is the union of sin and suffering, the removal of any evil by what is pure leads to an increasing dissociation of sin and suffering. Our suffering is increasingly the suffering of the repentant. We experience contrition or genuine sorrow for our evil, and yet because of a purity which absorbs our evil, we are better able to direct our attention to the places where God is secretly present.

Not only does what is perfectly pure absorb evil, it is not defiled by our own evil. Even though our evil causes Christ, who is perfectly pure, to suffer, it does not defile his purity. He does not return evil for evil, but instead endures it. Only those filled and utterly possessed by a love which is from above can so encounter evil and always act redemptively. Unfortunately, what others see in us is usually not divine love and their evil is reflected back rather than absorbed. Hence the vital importance of the presence in our world of the Lamb who was slain before the foundations of the world. He is present in people so that through his purity they may respond to evil with good. He is inexhaustibly present as the principle of the very order and hence the beauty of the universe. He is tangibly present in the Eucharist.

Weil stresses that it is by means of attention that evil is removed; for it is by attending to those places where God is present that contact is made with purity. Each moment of attention really destroys a part of our evil, so that given enough time, we can indeed become perfect as our heavenly Father is perfect. That is, we can be filled with his love and have our will directed totally by that love. We have seen, however, in our discussion of the love of neighbor and love of the universe how difficult it is to attend to those places where God is secretly present. So Weil is not optimistic about the achievement of perfection in this life. On the contrary, as we have seen, perfect love in this life seems to be possible only for those who are afflicted and who still love, as did Christ on the Cross.

Perhaps the major barrier to attentiveness is our resistance to repentance. For repentance means the admission that we cannot remove our evil. It is to recognize that we must turn to God, or to put it another way, it is to recognize that we are evil precisely because we live apart from God and direct our lives as we see fit and not in obedience to him. Weil uses a fairy tale to describe our situation.

> In one of Grimm's stories there is a competition between a giant and a little tailor to see which is the stronger. The giant throws a stone so high that it takes a very long time before it comes down again. The little tailor lets a bird fly and it does not come down at all. (WG 147–8)

[127]

Those who strive to be good by their own strength are like the giant. They may be able to make great improvements in their behavior and personality, but, like the stone thrown by the giant, they are bound to the earth. Humility is the recognition that we cannot by our own strength and goodness enter another dimension. It is he who by descending gives us his purity to touch and thus gives us wings so that we may indeed rise above our earthly condition, by being relieved of our evil and filled with his goodness.

Efforts of the will have their proper place in carrying out obligations, and in doing those things which are innocent and so permitted by God. But to strive after goodness with an effort of the will is one of the ways we avoid God and keep ourselves apart from him. Such an effort, however demanding and exhausting, does not threaten us; for it does not require our surrender to God. We can remain "giants," stronger than other people, and certainly stronger than a humble little tailor who cannot even compete on those terms. But Jesus has plainly told us that to possess the pearl of great price, we must sell all we have. Only God can elevate us into his kingdom.

Weil did not live and write long enough to consider in much detail the implicit love of God as found in religious practices. Next to her treatment of the Eucharist, her commentary on the Lord's Prayer (also to be found in *Waiting on God*) is the most extensive. She says,

> The words of the Lord's Prayer are perfectly pure. Anyone who repeats the Lord's Prayer with no other intention than to bring to bear on the words themselves the fullest attention of which he is capable is absolutely certain of being delivered in this way from a part, however small, of the evil he harbours within him.[19]

Her conviction that religious practices can remove evil is not based on a theory but on experience. She tells us she had to limit herself to two recitations a day of the Lord's Prayer because its effect was so overpowering. So her account of *how* perfect purity removes evil, although impressive, is less important than the fact that attention to religious practices does remove evil and that we can experience this for ourselves. The theory came after the experience.

Weil is so original in her approach that she has sometimes been deeply misunderstood. For example, her claim that God has withdrawn himself and left us subject to an indifferent universe has been mistakenly taken to mean that he is *wholly* absent.[20] Frequently she is referred to as a "secular saint" and as a supporter of a "secular" holiness.

Clearly Weil does not mean God is wholly absent. As we have seen, she claims that we can love God because, on the one hand, he has planted a seed of love in us and so we are capable of loving him and, on the other hand, because he is present in our neighbors, in the beauty and order of the universe, and in religious practices. In making these claims, she has utilized the Christian doctrine of the Trinity. The Holy Spirit of the Trinity is love, and we have the capacity to love God because the seed of love, or the Holy Spirit, is at work in us. The Logos or Word of God, the second person of the Trinity, she believes became incarnate in Christ. In the parable of the sheep and the goats, Weil points out, Christ explicitly identified himself with the afflicted, and in the parable of the Good Samaritan it is the assistance given to an afflicted person which is used as the paradigm of the love of neighbor. The Logos is also the principle of order of the cosmos, an order which is radiantly beautiful. As it is expressed in the first chapter of John's gospel, "All things were made through him, and without him was not anything made that was made." Finally, it is the Logos who became man who is present in the Eucharist.

Weil says that God is absent because he has limited his power, but she says he is present in the world in weakness. That is, he is present only in love and purity. However much she may depart from traditional Christianity in her concern for those of other faiths, she clearly is not so far from it in her teachings on the implicit love of God as to be associated with the Death of God theology—or any movement that puts forward an interpretation which radically breaks with Christianity as it has been traditionally understood.

There is some basis, however, for considering Weil to be a "secular" saint and for having a "secular" holiness. She believed that Christian religious practices, for all their value, are limited to Christian lands. Additionally, even in Christian lands people are often alienated and estranged from institutional Christianity. For these and other reasons Weil greatly emphasizes the beauty and order of the universe as a way to gain access to God, and such access is even important for people who take part in religious practices. Weil believes it unfortunate that Western nations have lost touch with the spiritual significance of nature, so she expends a great deal of thought and effort on how symbols in our places of work might be connected with our sense of the presence of God in the beauty and order of the universe. She was not satisfied with the possibilities of this kind of connection for factory work, but she has several promising suggestions as far as agricultural work is concerned.

> The law of gravity which is sovereign on earth over all material motion is the image of carnal attachment which governs the tendencies of the soul. The only power that can overcome gravity is solar energy. It is because this

[130]

energy comes down to earth and is received by plants that they are able to grow vertically upwards. It enters into animals and men through the act of eating, and it is only thanks to this that we are able to hold ourselves erect and lift things up. Every source of mechanical energy—water power, coal, and very probably petroleum—derives in the same way from it; so it is the sun that drives our motors and lifts our aeroplanes, as it also lifts birds. We cannot go and fetch solar energy, we can only receive it.

Poetry like this should suffuse agricultural labour with a light of eternity: without it, the work is so monotonous that the workers may easily sink into despairing apathy or seek the grossest relaxations; for their work reveals too obviously the futility which afflicts all human conditions.[21]

This is only a sample of her extensive reflections on the relationship between human labor and the love of God, and I refer to it here only to explain how Weil can appear to be concerned with a "secular holiness." She was interested in relating all of our life to the love of God and, since we cannot always be in church, she thought that a great deal of attention to secular life was important, especially the connection between human labor and the order of nature. Perhaps I should also note in passing that Weil had some first-hand experience with manual labor. She had a year's leave of absence from her teaching in order to work in a Renault car factory, and later, during the Second World War, she worked in the vineyards during the harvest.

One other frequent misunderstanding must also be avoided. Weil stresses that we must become detached from all earthly goods if we are to love God, and that we resist self-renunciation because it involves not only suffering, but the death of the self. She even says that our response to God's love in creating us with an independent will is to surrender it by our consent to our "decreation." Her own austere way of life and controversial death also support the idea that she advocates a policy of self-destruction. Whatever may be true of her own life and whatever may be the proper interpretation of her death (I myself do not believe that it was suicide through a deliberate refusal to eat enough during an illness), her teachings clearly state, as we have seen, that the death of the self is a *prelude* to resurrection. It is the renunciation of one kind of life so that another might come into existence, although at the time of renunciation, we do not know that there is to be a resurrection. So many of her remarks, taken out of the context of her thought as a whole, indeed support the idea that she favors self-destruction. But the rejection of earthly goods is actually a rejection of the illusions cast by our desires. We mistakenly assume that fullness of life can be found by the satisfaction of our desires for earthly goods, so rejection of these does not imply a hatred of this world or of life.

Moreover, our implicit love of God prepares us for a visitation from God. Weil compares our waiting to that of a bride who awaits the bridegroom, an image she takes from one of Jesus' parables. The image of marriage is not an image of absorption; rather, in marriage we have two who, by their devotion to each other, create a common life in which they both share. They have one life, but they are two people, and the creation of that common life requires the mutual recognition that each is an independent reality. It is the same with our love of God. Our will is to do his will; we find our good in his service. But we do not become part of God and cease to be.

"Decreation," one of Weil's favorite terms to designate our goal of loving God, does not mean that we cease to be. Rather it means that we cease to live a life apart from God, the kind of life he gave us when at creation he relinquished his power over the creation. We are "decreated" when we consent to obey him, not because he forces us to obey him by his power, but because we love him.

In her notebooks Weil contrasts "decreation" with destruction as follows.

Decreation: to make something created pass into the un-created. Destruction: to make something created pass into nothingness. A blameworthy substitute for decreation.[22]

Perhaps her affirmation of human life is shown most clearly in her last major work, *The Need for Roots*. She distinguishes between what she calls the heavenly and earthly needs of the soul. Just as there is no substitute for the good that is God, so too there is no substitute for earthly goods, such as friendship. *The Need for Roots* is Weil's analysis of the earthly needs of the soul and to what degree these can be satisfied by the restructuring of government, in this case the French government. Among our earthly needs is the need for a country and a society in which we feel rooted, and in which we enjoy social and political liberty and responsibility. Part of the brilliance of Weil's account lies in the connections she makes between our heavenly and earthly needs, and her proposal for society is a result of this connection. We have not considered this important part of her work because our concern has been only to treat what is needed to understand her views on the love of God.

A CONCLUDING NOTE

Pascal, Kierkegaard, and Simone Weil have many similarities. All three stress the uniqueness of God. He is beyond the universe in a dimension inaccessible to us. We cannot perceive him with our senses nor represent him with our imagination, and he is beyond the comprehension of our intellect. It is precisely because he is not part of the universe that God is so important to us. Only he can give us fullness because only he is inexhaustibly full.

Because he is above the level of the senses and mind, any attempt to evaluate the truth of Christianity within the boundaries of science, philosophy, or history inevitably reduces God to the level of our comprehension. As a result, the God who is accepted or rejected is the God of the philosophers, as Pascal put it, not the God of Abraham, Isaac, and Jacob. This is often misunderstood by both those inside and outside the Church. For example, everyone agrees that we must have faith. But this is understood to mean that faith is necessary only because we do not have enough evidence to affirm the reality of God. That this is a mistaken understanding of faith is clear, for it implies

[135]

that should we ever get enough evidence, faith would be un-
necessary. But faith properly understood is, on the contrary, a
response to a revelation of God, the revelation of a reality which
is above reason. Faith in what is above reason is possible only
because of some action within us by God. Faith is thus not a
substitute for evidence but a response to God made possible
by him.

Each of the three writers shows us how we may come to
faith, since we must be open to God's action. Their accounts,
although alike in many respects, differ in significant ways. Pascal, for example, shows us our insignificance in order to contrast
it to our greatness, and seeks to show us that Christian truth,
by making sense of this paradox, illumines the intellect. Because
the mind is illuminated, people are willing to wait and pray for
God to give them faith. Simone Weil uses only one side of the
paradox, our insignificance, and claims that if we hold to that
fact with tenacity, simply because it is true, God will come to
us with the seed of love. This seed, if not expelled, eventually
grows and enables us to become devoted to him. Another significant difference is Kierkegaard's stress on the need to aban-
don the life of the aesthetic for the ethical life before we can
truly become religious. Weil, on the contrary, believes we may
receive God's seed of love by a recognition of the futility of
trying to gain fullness of life from earthly pursuits and possessions *without* passing through an ethical phase. The extensive
role Simone Weil gives to nature's beauty and order clearly set
her apart from Pascal and Kierkegaard, who concentrate almost
exclusively on the workings of human nature.

We are not required to say that one view of our spiritual
pilgrimage is sound and another one unsound. Consider, for
example, a road map, where we may find several routes to a

single destination. Depending on where we are, one route is more direct or more feasible for us than another. Thus the route that Pascal, for example, describes may be more feasible for one person than it is for another. It may also describe more precisely the actual route a particular person has taken than the routes Kierkegaard or Weil describe.

None of the three pilgrimages I have described is supposed to suit all of us. Even should one or the other of them not be particularly applicable to us in our journey, they may enable us to help other people in theirs. We can use a map that describes routes we ourselves have never travelled to help others to find out where they are and how to get where they want to go.

All three seek to help us find certainty. As Weil puts it, "In what concerns divine things, belief is not fitting. Only certainty will do. Anything less than certainty is unworthy of God" (WG 161). It is unworthy because our devotion to him is to be complete: we are to love him with all our heart, soul, strength, and mind.

All three writers are convinced that certainty is possible. We can experience a love which is not of this world but from above. This does not happen easily, but it may happen to any of us, if we follow one of the paths they describe, or the path shown to us by any of those who love God with all their heart, soul, strength, and mind.

> When we are eating bread, and even when we have eaten it, we know that it is real. We can nevertheless raise doubts about the reality of the bread. Philosophers raise doubts about the reality of the world of the senses. Such doubts are however purely verbal, they leave the certainty intact

and actually serve only to make it more obvious to a well-balanced mind. In the same way he to whom God has revealed his reality can raise doubts about this reality without any harm. They are purely verbal doubts, a form of exercise to keep his intelligence in good health. (WG 163)

NOTES

NOTES

1. This is the theme of C. C. Gillispie's important history of science, *The Edge of Objectivity* (Princeton: Princeton University Press, 1960). For the point about Pascal and contemporary working scientists, see p. 82.
2. See F 130. The numbers I use to cite each fragment are taken from the translation by A. J. Krailsheimer, *Pensées* (New York: Penguin Books, 1966) because it follows Pascal's classification and the order in which his papers were left, and also because it is an easily accessible and inexpensive edition for the reader to buy. References here on in are cited in the text as F(ragment).
3. I use the old-fashioned word "charity" for love not only because it is used by the translator of Pascal, but to suggest the fact that the Christian understanding of love is distinctive and is not to be confused with the many ways we think of love in our society, as we will see when we come to Kierkegaard and Weil. "Agape," a Greek word, has been widely used by theologians for the same reason.
4. See also F 389, 502.
5. See *The Gates of New Life* (New York: Charles Scribner's Sons, 1940), p. 195.
6. All references to *Works of Love* are cited in the text as WL, and are drawn from the edition translated by Howard and Edna Hong, and published by Harper & Row in 1964.

[141]

7. Anne J. Freemantle, ed., *Protestant Mystics* (Boston: Little, Brown & Co., 1964), pp. 26–7.

8. See Søren Kierkegaard, *Philosophical Fragments*, trans. David Swenson, rev. Howard Hong (Princeton: Princeton University Press, 1974), pp. 32–43.

9. Søren Kierkegaard, *Training in Christianity*, trans. Walter Lowrie (London: Oxford University Press, 1941), p. 31.

10. Ibid., p. 98.

11. It first appeared in France in 1950, seven years after her early death, under the title *Attente de Dieu. Letters to a Priest* and *The Need for Roots* are also important for understanding her attitude toward the Roman Catholic Church.

12. Simone Weil, *Waiting on God*, trans. Emma Craufurd (London and Glasgow: Collins, 1959), p. 35. Cited in the text as WG.

13. Simone Weil, *Pensées sans ordre concernant l'amour de Dieu* (Paris: Gallimard, 1962), p. 11. The translation is my own.

14. Simone Weil, "Some Thoughts on the Love of God," in *On Science, Necessity, and the Love of God*, ed. and trans. Richard Rees (London: Oxford University Press, 1968), p. 148.

15. "Some Reflections on the Love of God," ibid., p. 156.

16. Ibid., p. 158.

17. Ibid., p. 159.

18. WG 135. Friendship is the fourth form of the implicit love of God: "To these three loves friendship should perhaps be added; strictly speaking it is distinct from the love of neighbor," p. 95.

19. "Some Thoughts," p. 149.

20. See for example S. A. Taubes, "Simone Weil: The Absence of God," in *Toward A New Christianity: Readings in the Death*

of God Theology, ed. Thomas J. J. Altizer (New York: Harcourt, Brace & World, 1967).
21. "Some Thoughts," pp. 151–2.
22. Simone Weil, *Gravity and Grace*, ed. Gustave Thibon (London: Routledge & Kegan Paul, 1972), p. 28.